INSIDE THE BOOK

Meet the essence gatherer. Living in solitude in a driftwood cabin in the dunes, she enters the magic transformation of mythopoetic experience, and is shown the way to compile a personal *Book of Secrets*.

But when imagination and intuition meet in the dunes, things aren't always as they seem. Drifting sands cover and uncover events, treasures, and memories. She is challenged by her history and grasps for balance in the "live and let live" world of the California Dunites.

Metaphysics, alchemy, poetics and mysticism all play together in her private imaginaire, as life opens to a far wider horizon. With support from her friend Cath, and inspiration from Ella and Gwyneth, the essence gatherer soon finds a personal path that is for her alone.

ATTARS is an account of liminal events happening behind the scenes when a collector of essences writes her initiatory *Book of Secrets*.

"As I read through Carol Sill's new book, I became deeply intrigued with the downright originality of *Attars*. I couldn't stop thinking about it long after it was done. You won't have read anything quite like it before. It is brilliant and wise." - *Ann Mortifee*

Attars

Carol Sill

Alpha Glyph Publications
Vancouver, BC, Canada

Attars
© Carol Sill 2017

ISBN: 978-0-9783485-9-5

Cover Design by James K-M

Alpha Glyph Publications
Vancouver, BC

www.attars.shamcher.com

Come now, read easily, and listen to my series of songs.

They are dream lullabies, melodies from strange lands, songs of heart's yearnings,

all sung just for you.

THE CRYSTAL ATTARDAN

I went to the dunes to find and express the fine essence of a particular rose attar, to show the way of things.

In summers past, the rose garden was in full bloom. The intoxicating scent of roses drew lovers again and again into the garden. Each day was a rose given to the beloved, massing into a huge bouquet.

Summer ended. The garden emptied, pruned down to sticks of thorn.

Years passed. Through all the ensuing summers, lovers strolled the same paths in the evenings, their senses alive. In magical beauty the roses in the garden unfurled so naturally.

Lovers give flowers one at a time to the beloved, like tasbih beads on a string. Why are those delicate living petals of the accumulated bouquet crushed to mash? No longer individual blooms, not even individual petals.

All blossoms mash together in the metal alchemical equipment.

Colour is refined away, becoming pure transparency. Finally tears of the roses weep one drop at a time into a glass collecting-vial.

Scent pressed into greater service becomes the simple essence of all bouquets of all roses.

And then the crystal attardan is sealed.

On a short dark winter day the essence may finally be completed: the rose attar.

I began to understand that from my birth on through life all my senses are gathering and gathering extraordinary bouquets; exquisite, earthy, angelic, dark and light, blooming buds, rotting fruits, dry sticks, and wide trumpeting flowers too heavy for their tender stalks.

All sacrificed at the moment of contact, crushed through the Great Alchemist's esoteric procedures. Natural essences are fundamentally unstable, so must be refined repeatedly, purified again and again.

What is left? A stable essence so refined it is nearly imperceptible even to the spirit. Yet how do we know it exists? We feel it is so. This essence of all is symbolized on earth as rose attar.

I unseal and open the jewel-encrusted crystal attardan. Perfume escapes like a genie from an ancient lamp. It expands, enlivening every molecule. It fills the room with magical summer air.

This is the way the beloved returns the condensed essence of every rose to every lover. In a flash of the transparent evanescence of the soul, all waters within me shimmer to mirror its chemical configuration. My tears tenderly match the tears of those long-ago sacrificed roses.

We call it "Rose Attar."

Attar 1

CROSSING THE THRESHOLD

"Come, Enter and See"

There's the time of twilight, in the Dunes, in Oceano (Northern California), and it's winter and the sea fog comes like a heavy cloak the same color as the sand, the sea, the dunes, the breakers' rhythm...and you're blind and can't find your way...and your ear can begin to catch a deeper than the waves sound, like voices...it's so cold, and dark, you have no sense of direction; the voices of the Yeti rise and fall, too close—God, they're chanting something so ancient...and like a panicked fool, you're running from nowhere to nowhere and lathered with icy sweat. And then the wings of Dreamwood's owl brush against your forehead, softly on your cheek, and sobbing with relief, you stumble after his connection to home—the cabin of driftwood with its can of kerosene—and as he flits from shapeless dark form to shadow, and returns to brush your face with stoic perseverance, leading home, leaving the voices of the Yeti rising and falling,...the loneliest sound in the world, along with the wind.

—Daphne Dunn, from Dune tales told by her father, Shamcher Bryn Beorse

How it Began

I'd been staying at Cath's place for weeks on end, not moving, not going anywhere. Most of my friends had given up on me. I stopped the Interior Landscape work; the Essence Classes had ended in sudden disappointment. Although Cath tried to help me, I went back to my old patterns. I was laying around reading until the late afternoon, then felt agitated and restless between four o'clock and sundown. Unable to sleep soundly, pacing through the house in the night, wringing my hands and crying. Having small tantrums and letting minor frustrations lead to huge arguments, particularly with my mother but also with anyone who crossed my path, even our letter carrier didn't escape my weird wrath.

When I moved in with her, she didn't know what she could do for me. Nothing was changing, nothing was getting any better. Days became weeks became months, and although the seasons changed, my situation remained the same. By chance Cath came upon an article in a small magazine about health through nature. It listed many expensive programs and theories, but one article caught her eye. It featured a California doctor who prescribed sunshine, long walks, swimming, pure living by the ocean. He worked in a town close to the dunes. We got in touch, my parents helped, I went to him.

I stayed in a rooming house when I first got to Oceano. I wandered to the dunes, following my daily walk (prescribed) and daily swim (prescribed). Through the doctor, I met some of the Dunites, and found my cabin. The doctor said it was a good one, and kept tabs on me for some time at first. My parents were reassured and so was I. He introduced me to Ella, whose cabin, Moy Mell, was the center of the community.

There I began my true journey. I started collecting essences, and in my time there I wrote it all in my *Book of Secrets*.

MEDIA INTERVIEW: PRESS EVENT

The reporter from a local New Age magazine, *United with All*, was writing an article about the *Book of Secrets*. Since this was part of the publisher's promotion I had to agree. He came with a photographer, and we met in an old cabin.

"Here's the original notebook that was in the cabin when I got there," I told him. Opening the old handwritten surveyor's notebook, I pointed out marks on the page. "You can see that his account had been tightly written; it's almost cryptic. It just wasn't legible. His free-form spelling and idiosyncratic abbreviations and marks didn't help. He also wrote the majority of his surveys in an incomprehensible script. I worked on it while I stayed in the cabin, trying to understand it. I was determined to at least discern the English handwriting in his account. My determination paid off. Nested within it are what I came to call 'nuggets of experience' that act as nodes or connections for those who wish to go deeper."

The reporter flipped through the pages and passed it over to the photographer who took a few shots of it beside my own *Book of Secrets*.

"Can you tell me a little more here? What prompted you to begin your account with a reference to a strange and unknown arcane notebook?"

"The journey I was taking was my own version of something that seems to be embedded in our human condition. It was encouraging to find this strange old notebook in the cabin when I first got here. It seemed like a sign that I was on the right track, you know? It was definitely intriguing."

"Interesting coincidence."

"You can imagine how I felt at first, worn out and unsure, arriving with only a few clothes and basic possessions. I stayed in the town first, just to get my bearings and check in with our friend, the doctor. Soon I left my bags at the rooming house in town, and set out every day to the dunes to look for an empty cabin."

"I know from what you told us in your book, you were in luck, one came your way. Can you tell us a little more about those early times?"

"Sweeping out mouse droppings and washing it all through and through. Bringing in a mattress, food and other necessities. The stove worked! Things like that. It's all in the book, actually."

"Getting back to the surveyor's account: how do you compare it with your own book?"

"There's a mention of the surveyor's account in my book, but otherwise they don't overlap much. It seems to me that they cover different territory."

"Well, his notebook was written in the past."

"True. I was fascinated to find it, but my own interest was quite different, as you can see in my book. Also, his notebook is very short, with an abrupt end."

A pause. In the silence the photographer moved in the background, capturing images. Then the reporter asked:

"But getting back to your own book. How do you feel about bringing your story out to the rest of us here in the everyday world you seem to have left behind?"

"I'm really happy about it, and I hope it can be understood. This quest was an inner task that took a lot out of me."

"From what I've seen of your *Book of Secrets*, it gave you quite a bit, too."

"Oh absolutely, I'll be spending the rest of my life unpacking the meaning I gained in this time. To tell you the truth, the book isn't even half of the story. But it is a start."

The photographer moved between them to take a few photos in the brilliant backlight at the open doorway.

6

DIARY ENTRY: VISION, INCOMPLETE NOTES

In the first weeks after Cath joined me, I found these notes beside the lamp on the table, but I couldn't recall who wrote them or what they were about.

Each day, a diary of one essence. Why? To understand its voice. Essences speak. How? Through collecting and taming the spirit of each.

Putting together bundles here, but it all happens on the other side at the same time. That is what gives your bundles their powers.

There is a warehouse of bundles that can't get to earth.

Opened in groups, what happens to them?

Too much information gets into the water supply, bringing accelerated transitions.

Last time this happened the wise ones convened to gather the scattered essences back together again.

The night before, she and I had been talking about the work and how to form an essence diary. Now I *do* remember that. But the other part about the warehouse of bundles, this is all news to me, and she had no recollection either.

But I'm getting ahead of myself here.

FROM THE SURVEYOR'S NOTEBOOK

These are the first lines I was able to transcribe from the original surveyor's notebook:

"Today, the sacred day of quiet, is the day I am destined to meet my new people, those who are coming near me to bring their stories and their wisdom.

Yes I may do battle. Yes I may be inspired. Yes I am ready to contend and do as was first intended long ago.

For the saga song lives on within the pulse of the heart's beating, awakening to the essences of old.

They wait beyond time's gate and past our puny sun. The glinting gold of their helmets reveals their whereabouts.

Here we find them camped and waiting the call. Here we see them at the fires, at the gates, in the tents, with the horses, near the playing zones.

Here the women stand still and listen keenly. They turn together and point in one direction: the east.

As I, too, turn to the east, I hear the clamour of weapons and armour. They are riding to the north. When I turn back, they have all gone, leaving only smouldering campfires in the light of dawn.

Warriors, women, sagas, old gods.

At my feet I see a flash of light. I stoop to pick up a rare and ancient finely-made golden coin. One side shows the profile of a man, the other bears the imprint of laurel leaves. I put it in my pocket.

As the sun rises on this unknown plain, I head towards it, to the eastern lands beyond.

I already know that these are not lands but interior places, the survey work has now begun."

FROM THE *BOOK OF SECRETS: ADVICE FOR ENTRANTS*

How does an essence collection begin? At first it is simple. You see a light or vortex of interest beam out from an object or substance. As you zoom into it, concentrating to the exclusion of all else, it becomes even more interesting and compelling. You soon become aware of emerging thoughts and sense new ideas, tracing its past and origins.

Then begins the process of breaking it down into simpler components. Core stories, elementary ideas, basic essences. Done correctly, each entry deeper into its primary simplicity compels you still further in.

It is as if you are being drawn into a cave with deeper and deeper passageways, until finally you reach a wide open area. This is where all ceremonies take place. Here is a hole above for light, with a hearth directly below for a sacred fire. You may see the essence objects lining the walls, represented in abstract figures that infer their core being and purpose.

There are many such caves. All are entered by going deeply into one thing, to the exclusion of all else.

Remember: going into any cave can take you further into the essence of the cave itself.

While reading this, I heard a wise one's voice.

"But that comes later. First your own collection has to begin. If you wish to understand, you have to find your first essence," the voice told me. "Discovering the essence is easy once you choose the first contact. But before that you will be tested."

I woke from my reverie and began this entry. I wondered: Had I actually heard that voice, or was it just in thought? And what had she meant by "tested"?

I was beginning my collection, and reading the works of others may not help me in that quest. I had to find that first essence, take that first step.

In The Forest of Offerings

I begin walking to the east in the light of the new-risen sun. To the left are fields and flowers, with a rolling hillside leading down toward the dry river valley. To the right is a bright birch forest with many flowers on the ground between these tall and loving trees. Their leaves rustle together in the wind as if they are singing, it is a fairyland moment. But I know it is imaginary. There is something more to find, something beyond this delightful opening. I sense there are other areas to expand that have nothing to do with this veil. The orchestral beginning is only a ruse, something to attract and tantalize but not ever to truly live in, for it is an illusion.

I see no noble horses looking through the tall tree trunks, no little elves and fairies singing songs of delight. No, that would be our own invention, the power of imagination, to cover something much more complex and perhaps horrible.

Beneath that meadow are the bones of many warriors, and it is their blood that has nurtured the birches. Theirs are the eyes that see through the bark, staring toward me as I walk upon their mass grave. For there is little here that is what it seems.

At sunset a reddish shape flits through the birch trees, almost like a flame or fiery one. It is not visible, only sensed, appearing at twilight. It sounds like a howling scream. It is without eyes, for its eyes are dispersed within the forest, and remain always captive there. It is not a safe place. There are old things here.

These are the guardians of the essences, and they are the dead. It would be a simple thing to turn away now.

I do not turn away, for I am traveling to the essences and so am compelled to leave the guardians an offering. In my bag I keep little things that may be of use sometime. Today I have some hard candies wrapped in twisted cellophane, some loose change, lipstick, tampons, a box of pushpins, a scarf, my phone.

I stick pushpins through the candy wrappers, fixing seven candies to the trunks of seven trees. Then I tie my blue scarf on one of the branches, and I say out loud, "Thank you for giving me safe passage. These things I offer to you now are in honour of your sacrifice. May you have peace."

Wind comes up and the glittering leaves of the trees flash together in sound. The blue scarf waves. I think of people who have died. I look up and now notice that offerings like mine fill the whole forest. Why hadn't I seen them before?

Cloths are tied to branches, bundles wrapped around the trunks of the trees, high near the crotches where the branches begin. There are all sorts of offerings and most look like they have been here for some time, exposed to sun, rain and seasons. I see an old suitcase rotting in the woods, a faded photograph, coins, sodden stuffed animals, a fresh package of cigarettes. In my body I sense contact from the many others who have been here before me.

A branchy path leads me to the top of the slight hill, where a pile of stones seems to survey the land below. Open to the sky, this mound seems significant. It holds many more simple offerings beneath and all around. A star Christmas decoration, a worn map, a novelty coffee mug, more cigarettes, candies, toys, pop bottles. Crummy stuff, weathered and wrecked, faded, looking like junk and garbage. These are our prayers.

A cloud passes over the sun and its shadow moves over the hill like the wide gesture of a great hand. It is a sacred moment.

Now the pile of stones reveals itself as a mountain of grey skulls: large and small animal skulls, and human skulls, too. Faces, teeth, caverns, forms. For an instant, they shine with an inner illumination. Brilliant blue-white light radiates from within them, they are not granite, not bone, but crystal.

All the offerings around them transform in light, glowing as gold and multi-coloured jewels. This timeless instant flows and extends through the atmosphere as the vision fades away.

I move on, aware. The guardians have accepted my offering and bless my journey.

I am protected. From this day forward I am permitted to be a collector of essences.

After a Dream I Give up the Interior Landscape Work

A wise one comes to me in a dream, saying that I had spent so much time here I'd forgotten my reason for coming in the first place. She shows me a specific mixture of ochre and animal fat for marking the sacred body parts. Primal basics.

I awake, vague and unsettled. Somehow I feel this was a message that the work I have been doing until now is in the wrong direction.

For one thing, I've been putting out a good deal of effort to understand life better, and to come to know myself more, or so I thought.

Cath had introduced me to the Interior Landscape Workshops, a successful women's retreat program: "An inner journey of self-discovery." We both went for an intro weekend. It was pricey, but we convinced ourselves that it was going to be amazing.

The brochure described it: "Placing their awareness on each body part in turn, participants find ways to understand themselves using a kinaesthetic language that bypasses the habitual patterns of the brain, to awaken new neural pathways and remap the body. Reveal the self in a way that is beyond psychology, to integrate the physical being and bring in a more positive outlook. Using tools like dance, journaling, drawing, and guided discussions, those taking part in the journey become able to transform aspects of self into a more cohesive whole."

We were thrilled to do these exercises, and it seemed like something wonderful was going to be revealed just around the corner. We had fun.

For example, focusing on the right hip, zooming in, could reveal the hip as a high hill that overlooks the landscape. This hill has a parallel one opposite, across the vast valley and the central river. The left baby toe is a little peninsula on the ocean shore, a small rarely-visited beach containing lovely foliage and an encampment of people who often visit the residents on the other peninsulas dotted along this shoreline.

Travelling this landscape through the mind in a state of yogic concentration similar to yoga nidra, brings up a lot to work with. Is everyone's right hip the same in their landscape image, or do they differ? Discussion in the group brings out all the similarities and differences, yielding greater insights along the way. We get a taste of discovering what is personal and what is transpersonal.

Going through the yoga nidra points of contact, the seeker moves the awareness to these locations, and from their resonance we create our own maps.

Stepping forward and moving to the right active side of the body, the map appears like this:

Moving down the right leg to all parts of the foot; as if traveling through rocks, plants, stone, paths, beaches and caves.

After the right side is "explored" (or imagined) like this we move on to the left side: a watery area, shaded, a mirror image with some differences.

Then to the back of the body where night travel begins.

And so it continues, through the back, the head and then internal organs. In this way, an entire landscape, now personally and poetically defined, becomes mapped to the individual body.

Movement and activity made innumerable variations. For example, placing the hands together, we noted:

Two rivers join in the forest, showing two visible streams. Stepping stones in the rivers make resting places on the rocks. Sometimes the streams narrow, but they are still visible. To each side of the joined rivers there are meadows surrounded by trees. Little rivulets all travel along stony creekbeds.

As you can imagine, the group dancing with this symbolic awareness was like a movement of nature's places and forces in action. To speak at the same time as creating the movements was quite poetic and beautiful.

I'd thought the Interior Landscape work was important, but the dream of the Wise One with the ochre made me question if it had ever been valid. Maybe it was only a preparation.

The primal firelight gleam of the ochre in animal fat glistened in my inner memory. The dream message directed me away from my self and my body as the location of the exploration. Cath and I talked late into the night about the dream and its meaning until I understood. That interior landscape work was, at the core, an imagined overlay. There is an innate natural map, waiting to reveal itself.

I felt catalyzed to seek the essences. I was to come so close to the pieces of the puzzle that there was nothing but that single puzzle piece, and then to zoom in closer than that, through the molecular and atomic structure to the finest possible bit of matter. Then from that bit of matter into the essence, an alchemically distilled simple.

But how was I to find a way to learn about that? The Essence Atelier had been a start, but a false start.

From *The Book of Secrets*: the Bundles and the Art of Distillation

In the ancient art of distillation, we discern the secret of the essence of things. There is a method of compression that enables the spirit to remain when there is no more substance, or as little substance as possible. The scent of roses fills the room where a saint has died, and these fine molecules in the air disperse to eventually embed themselves within all that had seemed so physical and solid.

As you may have guessed, the essences are not only from minerals, herbs, plants or animals. The finest are vibrationally-stored qualities that are unseen. Others may be aspects of the virtues, some ephemeral essences of the stars or planets as well as mysterious simples known only to the wise. These are often indicated in notation, symbol or talisman.

All essences are gathered into a sacred bundle. They are highly charged and have passed through many processes in relation to the time of day or night, phase of moon, season, breath of the practitioner and so forth. Molecular persistence retains the vibrational rays long after the original source has dissipated.

Our way of finding the essences and combining them came to us from long before the distilling of simples, but we have also used that method, too. We do our work with a Taoist method in mind, such as drawing in the essence of the tree using our metaphysical exercises to accept that essence into us.

We do this to gather within ourselves these materials. Soon we ourselves become, in some way, the bundles, the sacred essence carriers, the collection of all that is of simple harmonic meaning to us over our lives. At the time of death, the bundle is opened, then passed on to the next generation for safekeeping.

My own bundle has been opened several times in my lifetime. In the natural way of things, it usually opens at least during the death of a loved one, at a birth, while lovemaking, and when connecting with a worthy teacher or pupil. It also opens in certain other circumstances such as in nature, in the presence of sacred beings, in art.

When my bundle was incomplete, its opening meant little. What expanded from it was not useful to the world. Once I entered the realm of the sacred, new simples came to me for my bundle. Since that time, opened only rarely, it has been gathering power.

In trust we can receive bundles from others. I believe that no one can see what is in another's bundle unless permitted to do so. It must remain secret to retain its power.

When the holy ones gather to share sacred rites, these bundles are all opened and aired together. In a symphonic interplay of human and divine, our simples dance together in an atmosphere that doesn't diminish their power, but enhances it.

A magician's cabinet of curiosities, filled with extraordinary objects and items of symbolism and power, is not on the same scale of meaning and impact as the one little bundle which I keep close at all times. I always hold my collection of essences in this one small bundle, for safekeeping.

INTERVIEW: HOW IT STARTED

"Can you tell us how you came into this life and work?"

"I'd love to. You know, I didn't always know about these things. My book explains much more about how it happened, how I learned to gather essences, create my bundle, and enter the realm of those who wish to know."

"In your book you mentioned the dunes?"

"Yes, it all really started in the dunes. I was interested in essences and other esoteric lore before I went there. At that time Eastern religions fascinated me. I'd learned the basics of meditation and concentration but hadn't had the opportunity to go more deeply into it. I was looking for a place to do just that, but had no idea what I'd find when I got there."

She showed me a photo. "Was the cabin right here in this spot?"

"Yes, I believe so. It's so hard to tell now the sand has covered everything again. I recall it was here in this cove. Back then, what I first found here was just an old empty shack of rough planks and driftwood. It had the worst of the bed frames because other residents would lift the best bed frames for themselves as soon as someone moved out. So it was slim pickings since they'd all ransacked the place.

There was some clever shingling, with decorative clamshells along the rooftop; I remember how they gleamed in the moonlight like a string of lights. Later someone showed me how to collect tar from the beach and use it to stick the shells and other decorations to the cabin.

They told me my predecessor had fallen in love and was elegantly driven off to LA by an older woman interested in the occult. It seems they discovered they had been lovers in the time of Egypt and there were further mysteries to be explored. But that communion could only happen at her place, in the Hollywood Hills, where her comforts and passions could be fully enjoyed, without the peering eyes of hoboes and nudists."

"Did he leave anything behind?"

"Just some half-completed sculptures of wood and bone, along with a collection of vintage movie magazines, some basic kitchen stuff and a couple of dubious cans of food. And the *Surveyor's Notebook*, of course."

"Sounds like you had quite an adventure."

"Well, frankly, I thought to myself many times: What the hell am I doing here?"

"I'd heard it was a man's world out on the dunes."

"Yes it was, I was one of the few women living there. I had some cash from my savings, and a bank account back home. And my family to tap for help if I needed it, but I knew no one here except the doctor, and he was in town."

"Still, eventually you settled in?"

"Exactly. Once I was there for a few nights, I began to call it a cabin, not a shack. Abandoned, it was a shack. Later it became my home."

FROM *THE BOOK OF SECRETS*: THE RED ONE

He sprang from fire. He is as destructive as fire. He hid for eons behind all that is visible and he licked with flames all people to make wars. His eyes are red, his face is hard and black. His body is red, and his hands are red. He is wearing nothing but a swirling cloth around his waist and loins. He was not always this way. He is now drinking blood and he is now crowing and howling. His being is not animal but human, a darker form of the human that is forever hunted, hunting, hiding, and attacking from unseen places.

He loves to live near the dead warriors, and his strength increases whenever a warrior is killed, or is killing. We appease him with blood sacrifice. We see him at night. He was once like us, but he contorted. The son of the first of many early beings, he was not in form at that time.

We brought him into form because we needed to know. He is the great question why, and he will never have an answer. He kills all who cannot answer why and he then howls in despair. Like a rapist who cannot be satisfied even after the rape has begun, he will always remain in the intense suspension of unsatisfied desire without end or release. Death cannot appease him. Nothing can appease him. Nothing can destroy him.

He will always be, flitting through the birch forest, or lying at the bottom of the sea trapped in bitumen. When he rises, our world and the moon collude to make destruction. When he subsides, we imagine there will always be peace.

He wakes to feed. His anger is boundless. He has conquered all warriors and giants. His abode is in the dark oil, in the flaming gas, in the dead places. He has devoured his own family and has spat out their bones upon the graveyards. He loves nothing. He doesn't pay attention, for he is dancing all the time, lurching and dancing, devouring and howling. He is not a demon. He is older than anything else, for he has seen us throughout the eons. He came in a dense meteorite from the stars and he has all the time in the world. He can't sleep and is ever wakeful. Do not ever imagine he isn't there. If you are aware of him, he thrives. If you are unaware of him, he thrives. He sucks electric waves as if they were blood from the body of life. A drum can keep him at a distance. It is good to make a circle, he cannot come in when there is a circle of good people. Then he only hovers behind a little, looking in.

Yes he can fly. He can appear. He can disappear. His cock is enormous and brilliant red, always red, always hard, never satisfied, never released. He is red, his face is black.

He is also a woman, a devouring mother who eats her children, kills their spirits, and eats their hope. He gives birth to dark creatures and frightening spirits who attach to people to bring their souls to him.

His pattern is the maelstrom and the destructive chaos of that rim-spin.

Our alchemy teaches his uses. He has come to serve us, but first we must see him. Without him there is no world. He is our adversary.

FROM *THE BOOK OF SECRETS:* THE GOLDEN ONE

The incredible magnificent golden one has no equal. A being of golden eyes, innumerable golden eyes, all blissfully shining on all she sees, and she sees all, throughout all time. Gold came in balance of the red, and is a transformed version of the red. The golden one has an open face, is as delicate as a flower petal and as sensitive as a finely vibrating high string on the elven harp that has never been seen or heard since the early days of time. Bliss and joy are all, and an exquisite fragrance fills the air even at the thought of this one. Tears of joy and compassion flow continually from her eyes and love melts in her being in an ongoing orgasmic stream of life. Understanding and empathy meet as rivers in her expansive heart, and her many arms embrace all without hesitation.

She showers wisdom to all who wish to see her, and she has existed for all time. Her being will never be extinguished for she lives and draws her strength from an unseen source within herself and it is never exhausted. The maelstrom of chaotic life is calmed in her name which brings a deep peace. She joins with the sun and the stars and planets to enlighten all beings. She joins with the moon to moderate the fierce fire of the red one, whose love can only take the form of hate. She is larger than any being and finds ways to bring bliss even to the darkest night. Her penetrating gaze radiates pure love in a laser-etched pattern of divine symbology and causes the birth of all written languages and image symbols.

She is not a god, she came before the gods. Her voice is a song, her thought is a song, her dance is a dance of pure joy. She needs nothing, she gives everything away in radiant expression and still there is more, for she is a fountain of continual bliss.

She gives birth to all the gods and goddesses that are known and unknown to the world, in all times. In this female form she nurtures the world and all humanity. Contemplation of the golden one brings golden light to all.

She is also a man. His pattern is an interdimensional illumination that moves throughout time as a crystalline structure of the finest form of light, luminous and everlasting brilliant permanence.

Our alchemy teaches her uses. She has come to serve us, but first we must know her. Without her there is no world. She is our ideal.

From *The Book of Secrets*: Waters of Sun and Moon, Experimental Account

For a time I was collecting dew in early dawn, before the sun's rays hit the ground. It was a commitment and an experiment. I had to train myself to wake early, which I'd already been doing in my meditation schedule. My morning: wake, meditate, breath practice, gather dew, begin the day.

After gathering the dew, at dawn I added some of it to drinking water. Covering the top with a muslin cloth, I placed the glass where it would receive high sun rays at noon. Then at four o'clock, before the rays diminished and became more moderated, I took the glass indoors.

I took to drinking sun water every evening. It seemed to have a refined vibration that I believed would invigorate me and keep me healthy. It kept for a few days under the muslin cloth. No doubt it was less active than it would have been if it had been fresh, but still I thought it probably was better for me than plain well water.

One restless full moon night, I got up from my bed. I greeted the moon in the window, then uncovered my glass and took a drink of the water. Moonlight caught in the glass as I lifted it from the windowsill. I sipped the moon reflection refracted in the glass, pouring sparkling light into me. "Moonshine!" I laughed to myself.

There wasn't always dew each day, but it seemed to me that in the season when the dew is heaviest, we may need to drink more of the dew-water to maintain equilibrium. I didn't really know, but this was part of the experiment. Real moon water was actually dew, or star water as I called it. Later I heard that it was named "stars' tears" in other lands.

After some time of carefully notating all the variations of moods and meanings in my notebook, I realized that I hadn't ever really sensed in my physical body any change whatever from drinking the sun water. I only did it because I believed that it was probably true. I was thinking that my vibration may yet be too gross to perceive these natural subtleties which I knew were present even though I couldn't perceive them with my senses. Intuitively I felt this was a positive thing to do. At least I was up early, in touch with the rhythms of the day and night, and alert to their infinite changes. Did my experiment fail, because I didn't notice any direct change? I can't say now. I certainly felt righteous and good while doing it.

Cabin Days

I'd found a weathered notebook in the cabin's makeshift cupboard. It was with the movie magazines on one of the shelves below the wood plank countertop. Shelves lined the entire cabin interior: above the sink, above the bed and along all the walls. It looked like somebody had lived here long enough to really settle in. Later I saw the remnants of a pretty good garden, with flowering, fruiting and ripening perennials and self-seeding volunteer annuals coming up here and there through the weeds.

I didn't garden that first year, I was too involved in the inner concentrations for that. Or so I thought. I got my vegetables from town, not so much bought as gathered. With so many market farms and fields nearby, the train station was the best place to find free fresh food. Older Dunites showed me how to go to town with two sacks, not one. They told me to stop by the depot on my way home from the store. At the right time there were always loose veggies that had fallen off their pallets as they were loaded onto the train. There for the picking. So, filling the extra sack, I walked home looking forward to fresh salad. I made vegetable stew that night, and ate it daily, adding to it as it went down until finally the time came to head into town again.

In the small beauties of everyday life and the quiet solitude there, I began to learn the rudiments of real concentration and breathing practices. With constant attention I began to see results. My dreams, when they came, were active and vivid with meaning, but they were not always easy. Often I was working out karma all night, waking in tears or in a sweat. Day by day my body became more relaxed and my face became more innocent and clear. Tensions were gradually replaced with gentle well-being.

Mornings, I would sit with my cup of coffee to look out over the dunes, marvelling at the subtlety of colour and forms. Leaving my cup on the steps, I'd then walk out to gather more driftwood for the stove.

I often thought of Blake's words about infinity in a grain of sand and eternity in an hour. They were true. As I gazed out at an infinity of infinities, the innumerable sand grains were a glistening collection of secret diamonds. Time stood still. That blissful life would continue forever, but it existed in parallel to my past life involvements in the world.

At first I was afraid that at any time I would be torn from this unity into a vortex of confusion and darkness. I dreaded a telegram that someone in my family was dying or a letter from someone I didn't ever want to hear from again, or a bill collector finding my whereabouts, or an unexpected accident or illness.

In clouded dreams I saw myself in earlier homes, images of working at a store, my father embezzling, a stillborn baby, slapping and hitting. People I didn't know doing mysterious things. Running fast into the house to slam the door, only to turn and see a dead bird in the hallway. Some nights I woke frightened and crying, the wind clapping the loose shingles, clanging the wooden outdoor chimes, the whole cabin shaking as much as I was. There were foggy mornings into which I woke with the old restlessness, feeling captive and unable to do anything at all. But daily and eventually, this visionary parade of embodied emotional events became calmed by meditation practice and breathing. Or was it by the influence of the "Guys"?

The Guys

I dreamed I was making patterns using objects and foods. I was singing and calling out names, wrapping dolls in red cloth, burying them all. The ideas stayed with me, wouldn't leave me be. I decided to do it, as another experiment, in the evenings. So I started making figures out of dough, little dolls a bit larger than my hand. I baked them to hardness in the cast iron pot on the stove. Then I painted and decorated them with whatever was around: food, plants, wax, cloths, paints, wool. Soon these little figures lined the top shelf, like a frieze. I gave them all names, and numbers.

Later I realized it wasn't such a good idea to make them out of flour. I noticed one had been bitten into, then another; they were providing a feast for the mice. I might as well have deliberately set out food for mice with these little "Guys" I'd made. I had to get rid of them. So I gathered all these beings I'd carefully crafted and put them into the fire. Singing as I did so, it became my nightly ritual of breaking with the past.

Each time I tossed one into the flames I felt like I was a great giant goddess commanding a cleansing of the universe. Each one burnt totally. Some I had covered partly in wax, others I had oiled to look shiny. These burned most brightly. The ones covered with coffee grounds flared in colour, the ones with sand just smoked and smouldered. One burned entirely but left behind two blue beach-glass eyes in the ashes.

When I'd first seen the mouse bites I cried, then told myself I'd make new ones out of clay, better and more lasting. Now I changed my mind. What's gone is gone. Not ever replaceable. I could never replicate the crooked smile of little Jimmy or the wide creepy stare of Miss Marpool, or the ancient wise feeling that came off the Faceless One.

So I watched each one burn, and as I did, I took in its essence. I wrote its name and number on my list. I added the numbers of them all together, thinking it might come up to something meaningful or kabbalistic, but it was just 724, not significant. Beside each name I wrote words for its essences, later I combined them into a poem, like a dedication. The whole poem, lost when I moved, now remains only in memory. Part of it goes:

French fearsome tiny Aztec baby
Lilting scary innocent happy puppy
Stormy empty grateful tears god
Crybaby deadly astonishing teddy
Explosive fretful old dolly

Each line covers the duration of one burning. The words I wrote and felt during the burning weren't much like what I had thought when making them. The words describe the relationship with the doll and the fire, they are the words I sang and felt as each figure was burning. Then I wrote it down, before going to the next. I needed, you see, to collect its essence somehow.

I called them "The Guys." It took me many nights to make them, and it took as many nights to burn them all. I still see their faces in my mind's eye, and a few of them appear in my dreams, even after all these years. I never see them as they were in the fire, but whole, lined up on the shelf, all there, neutral, looking straight ahead.

I didn't plan how I'd make them, just let my hands and intuition work together. By the time one was completed, I had ideas for the next. As a final step, I dipped the feet in wax and then into sand. They still didn't actually stand up, but I could lean them against the wall. A newly finished one stood in an important place on my table for that night. I lit a candle by it, had a sip of whiskey or wine (if I had some) after I had put a drop or two on the new Guy to bless it.

In the flickering light of the dark cabin, it must have looked spooky to anyone peering in. But no one did. No one was nearby to see, or to hear my humming and singing. I wrote its name and number on my list and I contemplated each Guy's essence. Little Coy-Boy Sweetie Pie (#12) showed me one essence when he was first made, but this was very different from the essence that leapt to mind with the flame as he burned to become French fearsome tiny Aztec baby.

Feathers stuck with wax, lipstick for red mouths or cheeks or wounds, soot for short hair or eyes, or faces, or hands, or bodies. Coffee grounds, leaves, herbs, spices, all stuck on with wax or honey, or wrapped in fabric strips, thread, or wire. I shouldn't ever have used the honey. That was stupid. I only did one, and had the wit to take it outdoors right away. I laid it on the ground, to the left of the cabin. It was soon completely covered in ants. The next few days, the decay fascinated me; crawling with the ants and weathered, opened by the pecking birds, this little sacrifice tipped me off. "Oh no! Animals! Mice!" I rushed to the line of guys. Sure enough: mouse bites.

No time for my fine meditations and contemplation. I had to air out the cabin, clean thoroughly. I admit I didn't clean enough. I wasn't ready to kill the mice but I did want them gone. Or if not gone completely, at least managed.

I saw them run and jump in the corner of my vision. I vigilantly secured all food in tight glass containers. What was it they used to say: "Trust in God but tie your camel?" I was really tying it down. Batten down the hatches, mouse storm on the horizon! I became like the farmer's wife with a carving knife, ready to cut off their tails. Fierce and watchful, always on the lookout.

Sniffling and feeling sorry for myself, emphatically thinking once again, "I'm not cut out for this kind of life," I readied myself to do the deed. I stoked the fire. Soon the mystery of this action swept me into itself, and my role in it expanded in meaning and scope. With each step of preparation I went further into the significance of what I was doing. In fact "I" was far away, more and more an observer, as the fire built up, and the lamp brought near to the paper and pen, the whiskey opened and sipped with drops offered to the fire, then to the first Guy. I threw him in, watching intently as the flames engaged and finally engulfed the figure. Like an alchemist keenly observing all the physical transformations, I almost expected to see a phoenix rising up. But that was only fancy on my part. My fire-scrying showed me images whose word essences I hummed, spoke and sang before dutifully noting them. The next morning, my page was covered with ordinary words, it almost could have been a shopping list.

But that night, as I was writing them between the flames and the lamp, those words were etching the page with fire. Written from a tongue of flame, they were an illumination connecting to primal meanings and universal code.

From the *Book of Secrets:* Colours in weaving and painting

Weaving together basic threads to create the tapestries was the work of the women. On the edge of the encampment were the summer dye vats, used for generations, and the wooden drying racks that stood nearby.

We stacked rough wool in the shelter until the correct appointed day, for dyeing, spinning and weaving were all done in strict seasonal accord with the patterns of nature and changes in weather and light. The wiser older ones knew the signs and named the days on their marking hides.

We made our colours in friendship with the various herbs and substances that we gathered. We pounded, heated and treated them in the time-honoured ways. The correspondences between the spirit of the plant, the colour of the dye and the place of that colour in the pattern were all codified in ways that we passed on from generation to generation. We knew most of the plants that grew in our areas, but we could never be sure that the next location would have the same plants. When the people travelled, following the herds as we often did, we brought our dyes along in essence form, or as close to concentrated essence as possible.

Our sacred concentrates of colour hold the essences of our relationships with our plants, insects and animals. Our old ones guard these with great care. These essences are not for medicine or for pleasure, or for any other use. We use these only for colour, to create the patterns that show our people's ways, and to honour the special occasions in life with sacred symbols on our garments, hides and all the things we use each day.

Our art consists of calling to those who are near and far through our colours, shapes and forms. We use clays of differing colours and we decorate the clay with more colour, all to bring to the object its use and form in harmonic correspondence.

Let the concentrates of colour which are paints and dyes bring to life the secrets of our ancestors and our gods.

We make dyes for the wool, weaving materials, and hides. We make paints by concentrating dyes, and also by crushing sacred minerals. Sometimes sacred insects are also crushed, or bones or other parts of the animals that we live with. Our painters also learn special wisdom from the minerals.

They crush the old stones of centuries past, of the beginnings of our earth, to use as protection and power in our lives.

Our paintings hold sacred minerals in symbolic images to fix concentration and help us travel to far distant places. We fly that way, and the paintings act as maps and signs for the journey. When we all concentrate on the same image, despite time, we all meet there in that place, through our intuition. It is a sort of magic. The form without the magical influence of the worked mineral mixtures doesn't help us fly. Such reproductions and replicas are interesting but empty.

Our minerals keep and reflect the wonderful contact that happens from the pouring out of the artist's life force into the container of the work. With the minerals, the viewer can receive essences combined in a harmonious formation. It is more musical and more lasting.

Whatever we make has always been done in this way and from this viewpoint.

Knowing the ways of the ancients helps us to understand this way of the essences. They come from another dimension or a previous time, to bring purity and clarity to a time of too much information and not enough meaning and understanding.

FOLK

The folklorist paused for a moment.

"I believe that it was the rise of the old folk beings in all the European countries that caused the wars in the 20th century. We revived them, revered them, connected to them through the arts. The Irish poets, the Rite of Spring, the German folk-soul, all rose into conscious awareness in a way that hadn't been known or felt for centuries. Industrialization crushed the spirits. It had choked and crushed so many by the 19th century, then came the revival. Not just folk-singing in the square in Greenwich Village, but everywhere spirits bubbled up from within the earth, all through the 20th century as the Western world was in the turmoil of birth pangs for the age to come."

DIALOGUE ON THE FAIRIES

When I shyly attended my first community meal I found myself listening and observing as conversation went on late into the night. Moy Mell, the main cabin, was the scene of many dinners where extraordinary visiting guests mingled with Dunites. In warm camaraderie, Irish whiskey was liberally shared before, during and after the clam stew. At this, my first dinner, heated talk on economics turned radically to a discussion on fairies. They all seemed familiar with this realm, but it was new to me.

Listening, as if to music, Ella said: "I've seen the gentle green waves that reveal the delicacy of the tender new shoots. Just listen ... These are the sweet vibrational messages from the land of the fairy, the Elven world of plant healing."

A visitor piped up, critically: "Oh these ideas have become overused in our current culture. Why on earth do you persist on bringing up these old ideas that don't actually progress the work forward?"

"Because they ask me to. And I want to bring them with us, they're part of our heritage."

And then they were off, the dialogue in full swing...

"I heard that these are only a few of the innumerable races, species and beings that have existed on earth and in space for all ages."

"That's right. The old stories often tell of humans seduced by fairies, staying 100 years with them, leaving all behind in the twinkling of an eye."

"It can still happen even today, believe it or not."

"Oh I believe you."

"I've heard their singing. It's so compelling I find it hard to resist. Once I went closer, to hear better. I was certain there were words in the bell-like sounds. I thought for sure I heard my name being called. Then the next morning, I found a broad leaf with three lovely berries set on it, at my doorstep, left for me like an offering."

"Did you pick them up and taste them?"

"No, something warned me not to. I lifted the offering up in the palm of my hand and a bird swooped overhead just at that moment. I took that as a warning so I thought I'd better just leave it. So I took the leaf offering and carefully set it down on the grasses."

"Good for you. Those may have been the sleep berries and it would have been hard to resist them. Once you're knocked out, then the fairies come and spin their gossamer around and around you like a sort of cocoon and transport you to their land while you are sleeping."

"But why? What's their purpose?"

"We don't really know."

"It's in their nature."

"Some are just mean, some want to punish humans."

"Or they are curious."

"Others have been known to fall in love with us."

"A strange way of showing it. I'll keep away. But I do love hearing their music at twilight."

"Oh, we all do."

"And seeing the lights moving over the flower meadows on summer nights, so beautiful."

"When I was a child, I saw one who was graceful and beautiful, and I went close to him. But when he smiled to me he showed teeth that were pointed just like a raccoon's. I ran home as fast as I could. *Ha ha*, I heard his laughter following behind me as I ran. From then on I have respected all of them and kept my distance."

Ella laughed, and the talk moved on to gossip about old Dunites who I'd never met. I excused myself and walked home to my cabin. Under the brilliant stars, hearing the sound of the sea, wandering a little, I soon found my way.

OLD LORE, DIARY ENTRY

Looking now at my own involvement; how did she come to teach me some of this old lore and why did I agree? She appeared unbalanced and yet, there was a strong lure of wisdom and besides, what else did I have to do? I went to her cabin whenever she came to stay. From her I learned to hear the sounds in the grasses in the dunes, and although she could hear the orchestra of nature, I wasn't able to do that yet. She couldn't teach me that before she went back to her new home high in the hills. Or wherever she eventually stayed. A brilliant light unusual, Ella, the virgin Titania.

The simple act of writing this account will be my full inauguration, or so she told me. But she didn't know I also had other purposes that were my own. It was just that she was the only other independent woman there, and I longed for feminine company. The men were fun, and we had so many good laughs and serious discussions about economy, politics, energy, spiritual practice and discipline, gurus and teachers. Lily was around most of the time I was there, good for a chat over coffee, but she was mostly doing things with Peter and I didn't want to be in their way. He didn't speak much English, and was often brooding.

We kept company with the poets of old, reading about art and the individual talent by Eliot; we dived into all the influence of the others who had gone before! Not only did she bring in Yeats and the Irish independents in their full glory, her friends brought in Whitman and Carpenter, with all their expansive awareness and high sensitivity. So these ones were all engaged fully with us. When I go now to Moy Mell in my mind and heart, we all meet there, and we are all One. We renew one another.

She nodded off to a troubled sleep one night, and had a vision of little demons.

Next morning she told me, "The little fire demons were darting over the dunes in all directions, making exuberant sounds that drowned out the sweet songs of the grasses, sands, eucalyptus, sea, and sky. They stirred figure eights in the sands and they erased the old power vortexes. They made arabesque patterns on the ground, they never stopped moving. They ran around together in gangs."

She had no way to stop them, for they were doing all this in the future, long after she had died. Giant dune bugs. "More like dune buggers," she said to me once, after having had just a little more Irish whiskey than usual. Now

I've lived to see the truth in what she intuited: noisy dune buggies swarming the sands. It is now a recreational area.

In a dream, she told me: "The spell of the unified treasures may seem to have faded but Universal Spirit is always acting on its own here. There is always more than meets the eye." I see a flash of the old Gaelic cauldron, like the Cups in the Tarot, just before I wake.

CITIES OF THE DEAD

My time in the dunes, in my cabin and the cabin in Moy Mell: it is all a city of the dead. Moy Mell's name is my clue, the pasture of honey of all the poets. The dead poets' afterlife. Is this where I am?

All differing times and places merge together. The past, present and future infuse one another. Here in the cities of the dead, can the future infuse the past? I believe so. Time is only one sliding variable in a multiverse of potentiality. Events stand alone and yet encompass everything in simultaneity. For a flash, when events occur within the illusion of time, a story makes sense.

And all the while, everything that is dies, releases its essence whether crushed, burned, dissolved in chemicals, distilled. Carrying one essence while alive, it shows another after death. Which is the "real" one? Are we aware of our after-death essences while alive? Does this have anything to do with the soul or the concept of the soul?

The great sufi mystic Inayat Khan said we are collecting experiences to fill an akasha which is empty now, but that we fill with the essences of everything we experience in our lifetime.

As I explore the cities of the dead I see each akasha is a home. Someone else had left my cabin behind. I moved in to inhabit it for a time, then abandoned it to emptiness. Now it is covered over by drifting sands.

Thinking in this way, I thought I saw an old woman walking far out along the dunes, her hair long and white.

"The faces of pure being!" she exclaimed. "Did you see them? The clusters of babies, like bubbles, or eggs, or grapes. Waiting to be born." She raised her hands in wonder, arms wide against the sea.

RITUAL OF THE FOUR TREASURES

"Welcome to Moy Mell!" Ella welcomed us like a druid queen. It was nearly twilight. We had gathered early before the evening meal. A fire roared in the beautifully-worked stone hearth and the 12 of us were seated round. She set her clear eyes on each of us in turn. Her sword, cauldron, lance and stone, the four Gaelic treasures, glowed in flickering firelight.

"These are the legendary Sword of Light, the Cauldron of Plenty, the Spear of Victory and the Stone of Destiny, here in the dunes, brought from Ireland," she said. It could have been any time at all, in the distant early times, but it was now.

It wasn't the afterlife at all, either. We weren't the poets assembled in death to live forever in the fabled Pasture of Honey, just regular local Dunites who were living there at the time. She had poured us strong drink and gathered us to share in the ancient ritual of her homeland.

Earlier she'd witched a power vortex in one of the coves. There we were to meet the others and enact the ritual. She divided the 12 of us into four groups, one for each of the holy Gaelic treasures.

I was with the cauldron group, and the three of us stood together and held it. It was small, only symbolic, nothing at all like the big cauldron in the Scottish play. Still, it felt authentic, 100% cast iron, finely decorated. "Souvenir of Ireland," I thought to myself. The Pot of Gold at the end of rainbow, the meaning of the cauldron of plenty was like the cornucopia. The "plenty" in the cornucopia is all from the earth, and the Cauldron of Plenty includes magic gold and precious stones. It was ours to work with now.

She glided over to us, looking so otherworldly we couldn't imagine her living on the same earth. She was in her highest place, exalted beyond anything earthly, hearing her own music, attuned to the slightest shift in vibration. When she spoke and switched between English and Gaelic it sounded like an incantation, but nothing like the incantation yet to come.

We were working to save the dunes from development. A big company was buying the property with huge recreational development plans. How could so few of us stop that juggernaut?

We became solemn as we went through the door to walk down to the power vortex in our groups. We began to do exactly as she asked. It was a procession. She was the main conductor in our ritual, and her intense focus made us all cut out the wisecracks and chitchat.

We were no longer catching each other's eye to distance ourselves from what was happening. Most of us had meditated, but few had done any kind of ritual. The feeling was new and unfamiliar. We were children taking first steps into the forest, following the sound of the piper who lured us ever deeper.

We arrived. She rang the bell three times. Then looking up to the oncoming evening stars she began to recite the lilting words. We soon heard more: an ancient growl, a fairy song, an elven imploring and a human plea. Her invocation drew them all toward this place. So these were the others we were to meet here in the cove. Not humans.

In the sand she marked a large circle. With her stick, still poetically chanting and talking all in Gaelic, she stepped inside it. We stood just outside that line, in our groups at our appointed cardinal directions: North, South, East and West, each according to our treasure.

She called us up in turn to place the treasure in the sacred circle. Her voice was so powerful it didn't seem to come from her at all, but from the combined voices of the owners of these ancient tools.

I felt faint and began to swoon as the whole scene melted before my eyes. Over us stood great spirits of old. The ancient ones of the four treasures each stood in place at their direction. Then it all melted further and they were on a high and hilly green mound looking out to sea. The spirits of old joined hands in the centre, in a pledge of some sort, and turned, becoming a circling vortex. Their feet lifted from the ground, they were spinning like a wheel. All that remained was the clasping of their hands, fused. A golden circle with the emblem of this unified force rose above them to become a sphere of flashing and blazing light, shining in all directions, suspended there.

A high tone rang through the air and I snapped back. I opened my eyes. There in the centre of the circle were the four treasures, and singing round and round inside the circle she was dancing and turning. Outside it we, too, were dancing. How had this happened? How did we know what we were to do? Was this a kind of madness? It didn't matter. With our arms up we repeated her calls and cries.

Then it was suddenly finished.

We stood solemn as stones, while she buried the treasures in the sand, covering the spot with the beautifully-worked cloth she'd brought from across the sea. As if commanded, we all went back to the cabin while she remained at the spot a little longer, sitting on her knees, rocking back and forth, softly keening and crying and humming.

Back inside Moy Mell we built up the fire again and set the lamps alight. Someone brought out the whiskey. We drank to our health and success, but none of us could mention what we had just gone through. About half an hour later, she came rushing back inside, wild-eyed and exhausted, ravenously grateful for the bread and whiskey we offered her. Seated in her chair by the hearth, beside her she placed the treasures, wrapped once more in their beautiful cloth. She began to speak.

"The storm is coming now. It is done. ... Now who will serve the stew?"

I dug the wooden ladle into the big stewpot on the fire to give it a stir before serving. We carried the pot right onto the table, beside the stack of ceramic bowls and spoons. Everything glowed. As everyone helped themselves we heard thunder in the distance.

The developers never did follow through in their plans. They decided the area was "too unstable" to work in, and chose another site, further down the coast, far from our dunes.

The Hanged Man

The troubles, when they came, took us all by surprise, as trouble always does. It was not that we expected our Shangri-La to last forever, none of us were that naive. But the shock of the death of one of our own ran through the group like a snake on fire.

Martin was the one who found him, hanging from a eucalyptus tree in one of the tenderest coves. His body had been there for about a week: the coroner from town gave the estimate. Stunned. How could we not have known, or felt it? We just stood there unable to make sense of it. The coroner and his assistant cut him down, and laid him on the ground.

Someone (who?) ran to his cabin to get things that had made him happy in life, bringing them to him. After the coroner filled in his notes, measuring the tree, figuring out the setup, we placed Pat's favourite things around him on the sand. Well, maybe not favourite, but at least familiar. When the coroner took him away, we arranged Pat's stuff around the base of the tree and went back to his cabin.

There we saw something we probably should never have known, something Pat never wanted us to know. He sure wasn't the meditator we'd thought he was. His cabin had been a mess, strewn with bottles, old smelly clothes, newspapers and just plain cruddy crap. Everywhere. It stank of old food and sweat and piss. You could hardly find his bed for all the garbage. Now he hadn't let any of us in for months, and looking around it was clear there was a big lot of trouble filling his mind.

Somehow when I saw his boots lined up by the door I was struck with sobs so deep, but I hadn't known I'd even cared that much for him. One of the hermits, and a prolific professional writer, his work still at his typewriter, words on the page in the roller there. They made no sense to me. They weren't even words, just strings of letters and spaces that looked like words from a distance. His papers covered the table and they were all like that. What the hell?

At the side, his earlier works were neatly stored in manuscript folders, all professionally titled with numbered pages and the word count on the first page. It looked like there were 5 or 6 of these folders.

"Oh what will happen to them now?" I cried again.

"You better take them for safe keeping. His brother's coming from the east and he'll want to have them."

We cleaned his place up as a way to honour him and because we didn't know what else to do.

"Why did he do this? How didn't we know?" I asked myself.

Our attitude of "live and let live," of radical self-expression and individuality; did it mean we weren't taking care of each other? Or was he someone who would have done this no matter where he was?

Maybe the eucalyptus cove with its finer vibrations was the perfect place for him to let go. Far better than a crappy apartment in LA or a rooming house dump in SF where no one would bother or care. But did we bother or care? Maybe he didn't want to be where someone would bother or care. More free that way. At least here in the sky and the sand and the beautiful dunes there was peace. No kids would accidentally find him. He was with friends, but at a distance, non-interfering friends. But should we have interfered?

That night we met at Moy Mell to raise our glasses in his memory. How he had stripped naked to dance around us at that best of parties! All hail! How he had laughed at the silly strivings of the town women who he met, took home but never saw more than once or twice. All hail! How he loved to walk the dunes. All hail! And we always came back to his writing. He hadn't had an assignment for a while now, and having been a well-known journalist this must have galled him.

"More time for my novel," he'd said, but we knew that was why he'd come back to the dunes this last time. Couldn't afford to live anywhere else, actually. Like most everyone there, if the truth be told.

Over the years he'd been in and out, changing his role from visitor to Dunite, back to the city to work, then back to the dunes, over 6 or 8 years now, back and forth. This last time he came and stayed, kept to himself more. No wife or girlfriend this time either, just alone.

"I'm working on the most amazing novel. It's my life's work condensed and crystallized," he told us with a particularly excited look in his eye.

So we knew enough to leave him alone until he came out, just as we did with one another.

Next day, I went back to his place on my own. I read through his later pages that I found scattered on the table and stacked by the folders. The inspiration had turned dark, then darker. He had his narrator combing through bones and chewing sinew after horrible war mutilations, poisoned, confused. The pages began to repeat. They radiated profounder despair as they listed atrocities, ranted angrily at everything in life itself. These corridors of madness had no resting places, no doors. His last pages were incoherent. From page after page of detailed autopsy findings and minute descriptions of mutilations, the words began to shift into gibberish. It wasn't at all poetic, it was just a mess. Then came the lists.

Numbers appeared in the writing, peppered in places on the pages, and the gibberish pages took on the look of code patterns with numbers holding places in them. He'd tacked some of these later pages on the wall by the table, and drawn lines from one number to the other with coloured pencil. The patterns could almost have revealed meaning. But I didn't see it. No one else could make sense of it either. The lines showed no meaning to us.

Piles of unopened letters from family back east, an uncashed paycheck from a writing job 6 months before, sprouted potato vines, overfull ashtrays and saucers of ashes and butts, more whiskey bottles, fleas in blankets, soiled pants stiff on the floor.

"What if he'd been sick?" we wondered.

The fog in those days seemed to come from him, carrying molecules of his sorrow into our hearts. We were all caught in the fog of his deep sadness.

"I'm sorry," he seemed to be telling us, "I just couldn't do it anymore."

My friend the town doctor knew him well, and some of us went to see him and talk about Pat. Maybe he has an answer, we thought. When the coroner took his body into the van and over to the basement of the hospital, some of the men helped him. We never saw him again. His family from back east didn't come to his cabin, they stayed in town. We just cleared it out and did the usual holy smudging so it would be ready for the next Dunite. Someone painted a sign that said: this was once the cabin of Pat O'Hara, well-known writer, journalist and bon vivant.

We all knew he had a history of picking fights, and we knew that he found peace in the dunes. He'd been drunk, wandering the street in SF, and they sent him home to the dunes. He wasn't making sense. Howling in anguish, he came to the doctor in town, who found nothing physically wrong. The pain was inside his soul, something was burning there. The booze wasn't helping.

After he died, we avoided his cove for a while. We just left it to settle there, let the sands move over it, as they had moved over his cabin. The vibrations in that cove were never as they had been before he hanged himself. The gentle spirit of that spot had changed. No one went there, no one wanted to, not even people who didn't know about him.

We blamed ourselves, some blamed each other. Some were philosophical, some said their meditations were helping him on the other side.

"Good god, if the meditations could help him now, why didn't they help him then?"

"And why didn't we know?"

"Or bother to find out?"

The whole thing scared us. It could have been any one of us, and we knew it. We talked late into the night. Some talked of the Hanged Man in the Tarot, others mentioned Odin and the sacrifice at the world tree.

One said, "You know, I can sense the future in that cove, I've felt a transformation."

We asked, "Had he slipped into another pattern?"

"The numbers he'd typed looked connected to something besides each other; was it a pattern or sacrifice?"

"He never actually meditated, so when the energy hit, I think he couldn't handle the charge."

"That's possible. With no initiation, no protection from the forces he wasn't able to withstand the darkness within him and in the world."

"I don't think so. It was the whiskey driving him mad, making him crazy."

"It was just that he felt useless and hopeless; he'd run out of work, no one would hire him even with all his talent, and that's what killed him."

Our druid wasn't in the dunes when it happened, she was off on a lecture tour. She lived part time in a house with a friend, and lately had only come to the dunes when someone important was coming to visit, so she could show off Moy Mell and explain the particularly sacred vibrations of the whole area. She's the one who had talked of the sacrifice, early on.

But I'm still asking, "What for? Why?"

I think sheer desperation pushed him past his limit. I found a lot of rejection letters in his files, alongside the manuscripts of his unpublished novels.

On the floor beside his bed I found a well-worn letter dated two weeks before he died. It was from the paper he wrote for most regularly, telling him that there was no more work for him this time and wishing him the best of luck.

SOMEONE NEW

And so began the tender times of thoughtful sensitivity.

Meditations became more thoughtful and we started sharing them, often sitting together in twos or threes; ad hoc of course, and each doing something different in our own experience and training. After seeing Pat's parents who'd come from the east, along with his almost identical but bashful brother, we each contacted our own parents or families, some even went to visit on the quiet. I was glad I'd stayed in touch with mine, and with my old friend Cath.

Now the drunks couldn't keep this tenderness up for too long. Soon they were spending the days in remembering, crying into their rye, "I really loved that guy."

Some of them came round my place at night, to "comfort" me, but I'd refused them before so it was easy enough to remain as pals. I sent them back home a little more gently than before.

In a few months we were back to normal. With memory taking the place of feeling, we, too, began to live again. The sands shifted, and so did we.

A new person came on the scene, a breath of fresh air, right on time. He claimed the empty cabin, and began sweeping out the sand, clearing the doorstep. We saw smoke from the stove, and knew he'd officially moved in. A young sculptor.

Later the place was ringed round with his radical abstract objects, or were they figures? Or physical thoughts? We never knew, he never told us. They were kind of like vibrational vacuum cleaners. Sadness left the area, replaced by some inexplicable ideas from the future.

He kept to himself but we'd learned our lesson. One at a time, and on our own, eventually everyone dropped by just to say hi and show him the ropes of dune living at its finest. We never left him completely isolated. He could work day and night without distraction but our eyes were on him, just as they were on each other.

None of us used drugs much in those days, but he smoked "tea" as he quaintly called it. I remember him looking out at the dune colours at sunset, smoking his hand-rolled cigarette or his long white pipe from Morocco.

He'd travelled there and told us tales of the east. A terrific raconteur.

"I'd been travelling in Europe with Mother and her companion, Louise, who was also her best friend. We had a jolly household always on the move,filled with books, remarkable people, living in the arts and doing what we thought most mattered in life.

Then one day, Louise became smitten with a Parisian girl my age. They started including her in our outings, and for meals, then evenings. Soon they couldn't do anything without her. She was intelligent, but sullen. Her presence meant that a more serious outlook replaced our former laughter and sparkling conversation. Other friends stopped coming around.

"The Parisienne," as Mother and I called her with sardonic irony, was openly communist. She wore stark, plain, rough clothes. Her short hair and lack of lipstick gave her the air of a studious adolescent boy. I couldn't get along with her; she seemed alien and never directly spoke to me. Only to Louise. Her big eyes, staring at Louise.

Naturally Mother was more and more fretful, desolate and anxious as Louise became increasingly involved with the girl, who often slept over after the nights of talk and drinking. They stopped going to clubs in the evenings and went instead to lectures and meetings, returning home to feverishly discuss the events, implications and ideas until the wee hours. Eventually Mother went to bed alone, Louise stayed up.

When the time came to leave Paris and travel back to London, Louise resisted, insisting they stay and all live together in Paris. Mother knew that would be insufferable. Soon she and I left to travel in Morocco, not without many tears and imprecations through many nights. It didn't matter. What was done was done. Without mother, Louise had no income, and so became dependent on the girl, who revealed that she actually came from a wealthy family. They gave her a monthly stipend and an annual dispersal, but of course she despised them and their bourgeois middle-class values. I don't know if Mother ever heard from Louise again.

After Morocco, we came to America. By then Mother was bereft but philosophical. It wasn't long before she found another delightful friend to share the joys of life with. I didn't like this one much but it was such a relief to see her happy and laughing again. I hoped she'd soon reclaim her old self. Those days in Morocco were rough. Sometimes she couldn't get out of bed, or wouldn't, and the food didn't agree with her. Nor did the climate. But the sounds and smells and colours and patterns soon worked their magic, and got into her skin. Soon she was riding camels, smoking a long thin pipe (this very one in fact!) The whole experience!

Our little family, such as it was, had been shaken, but I was nineteen by then and already late for college. That's why I took off for a year of barefoot natural living before the regimentation and requirements of a so-called education. Time to join the Nature Boys!"

So it was that his mother's support brought him to the dunes.

I was fascinated to hear that he hadn't been a sculptor before this time, the idea just popped into his head one night as something to try. The magic of the dunes! His sculptures that year transformed the sorrow of desperation and suicide. Dark abstractions and "difficult works" to some, they were a saving grace for the dunes.

WE ARE THE ESSENCE NUNS

My old friend Cath came to the dunes later that spring, with Gord, her nineteen-year-old nephew, their little yappy dog, and her small library of accounts and experiments. We planned to spend the summer together, doing experiments and documenting them. We called ourselves the "Essence Nuns" and soon started to work.

In seeking the essences there has to be thorough documentation of each step, so the essence path could be traced down through the ages. Cath had been studying for a few years, so she'd seen some of the books by others, that was where she got this quote from: "And so they wrote their book together, the person who dictated and the one who wrote it down faithfully." She'd also replicated some of the basic essence experiments. I was still new to it, and was excited as can be when anything worked at all.

Mindful of our privacy, Cath set up her tent beside my cabin, holding it to the ground with heavy stones. Gord had fetched them from the rocky place by the train tracks just past the depot and carried them back in his pack. Gord's tent was over to the other side, a ways further from us. The little dog made a circuit path from his tent to Cath's to my place and back again. Camping in tents on the shifting sands wasn't so great, so we put together a tent base with some pallets Gord found at the depot.

"They were just lying there waiting for the vegetable farmers to pick them up, and we'll return them in the fall," he said. I didn't say no. I knew far worse had been done by the Dunites. He put each tent on top of this makeshift foundation and it seemed to help.

Gord liked to sleep out under the stars, and so did I, so some nights we all did just that. We even convinced Cath to join us, but she often gathered her stuff before daybreak to avoid the heavy foggy dew. She was right. Gord and I often woke in soggy sleeping bags with clammy wet hair.

It was great to have the company but I missed my old solitude, especially in the mornings. The sacred silence was now broken by conversation, the happy barks and growls of the dog, or just the rustling and bustling in the kitchen. Still, as I sat quietly contemplating the sunlight colouring the sands with its subtle changes from dawn to day, I soon learned to tune into these finer vibrations, and let the sounds fall away.

Gordon always got up later. Cath and I were ready to start and then had to hold back till she'd done his breakfast, which she always made for him.

Still! I told myself not to get involved and to bite my tongue as she served him like a little boy, this big lad man.

"I know what you're thinking," Cath said one morning. "But he's been so good to us over the years, and I miss my own little guy. I've got to mother someone," she laughed. Her own boy, Aidan, was spending the summer with her ex and his new family. Cath walked into town every other day to call them.

Gord was hardly a child, even though Cath thought of him as her little nephew. He was six foot, sun-browned, strong, healthy and happy. Soon he'd made friends with the sculptor and they started going into town together, meeting girls, Cath said. They were typical California nature boys wearing the bare minimum of scruffy old bathing suits and strong home-made sandals.

Cath and I learned to make the sandals from one of the old timers. She sent a few pairs back to friends at home, and made a smaller pair for Aidan. Everyone wore them. The sand was too hot on the feet not to have any covering, and with shoes there was so much trouble with the sand. We did clean ourselves up when we went in to town but we spent most of our time in blissful ignorance of our appearance in social terms. We wore bathing suits, sarongs, shorts and tops, with shawls at night. One or two dresses were more than plenty in case of emergency. Pants and sweaters for cool foggy mornings, a good hooded windbreaker for the rain and that's about it.

We didn't care how we looked. By mid-afternoon most days, with hair tied back, we were so absorbed in our work that we were skimming along above ourselves, taking giant steps around the globe, here and visible to others but functioning high above.

Moving our substances from form to form, compressing, distilling, diluting, notating. She'd brought her mortar and pestle, and a few other tools. A bunsen burner and gas. She was a better draughtswoman than I, so her notes were often sketches of the processes, or charts and diagrams. I wrote longhand in our main notebook, accounting each process and results in detail. I laugh at this now, knowing how useless such notation can be in this quest, but then I commend us for the serious effort and the dedicated concentration we applied to the tasks.

Often disappointed, we tried again and again. We concluded that many of the books she brought had proven to be bogus imaginings, even Albertus Magnus seemed farfetched, not even metaphorical. We weren't able to replicate either the steps or the findings. No worthwhile results at all. We might as well have been in the playground. Still we noted it all in good faith, and underlined the lack of expected result.

"It could be the expectation that's in our way," she remarked, but I disregarded that at time. I was convinced that this was a possible quest and that there were clues we could glean from the books of others who had gone before.

It was like the buried movie set from the *Ten Commandments*. The great 1920s blockbuster silent film whose flimsy pyramids and simulated Egyptian statues were left behind to be covered in the California sands. Uncovered, the sphinx and the other figures, the colonnades and thrones were revealed as only paste and wood, thin and insubstantial substitutes. They referred to the mysteries of ancient Egypt but were just a crude imitation of its surface, now covered by parallel sands of time on the opposite side of the globe. We knew there was an Egypt of the past, but this replica was no substitute, plus it was a ruin. That is what it felt like when we followed these books describing the essence process. I knew there had to be something more.

FINDING THE SCRYING JARS

Most nights I lit candles in the scrying jars, to read the patterns that projected onto the walls with natural shadows.

This process began when I dreamed of Lake Winnipeg and Lake Winnipegosis. I fly over those two sister lakes in southern Manitoba and see them connected by two rivers that feed them and are fed by them, like tubes. The rivers are called Mary River and Little Mary River. Lake Winnipegosis has been given a name that suggests something medical, but it is Aboriginal. Winnipeg is Aboriginal and so is Manitoba. Only the Mary Rivers are English colonial names. No doubt named by Brandon or some surveyor.

Mapping was the old fashioned way to fly over territories and see them at a distance, and on the map the lakes look like organs and the rivers look like tubes placed in them to irrigate and heal them from unknown imbalances.

After that night, I put two large glass fish bowls outside my doorstep. I filled them with lake water and put in a couple of goldfish from town. Half-buried in the sand, they were my private ponds.

The largest represented Lake Winnipeg. I'd see the flash of a golden fish in it from time to time. Through all that murky water, a flash of gold. There was a smaller golden fish in the smaller bowl, Lake Winnipegosis. My miniature artificial lakes were perfect, more perfectly round and deep, more precise geometrically than the natural lakes.

My private lake bowls were soon overgrown with murky bracken, so I netted the fish and took them over to the freshwater lake far behind the cabin. I kept two jars of the mucky water from each bowl on my shelf, and dumped out the rest.

When their water evaporated and the jars had dried out, I put small candles in them. In the evenings, the lattice pattern of the dried muck and murk flickered in projection on the walls. The projected shadows of leaves and straw, with bits of dried brown bracken, inferred natural formations. Scrying late at night I saw cities and landscapes of the past and of the future.

SUMMER'S END

Summer ended soon enough. Cath left some of her supplies behind so I could continue on. Gord stayed on too, living in the sculptor's cabin that fall. I saw him around but he was weightlifting most days, taking long running trips along the coast, obsessed with his bodybuilding. The taste for tea that the sculptor had left him with didn't seem to interfere with his physical fitness and love of the outdoors. He was a good sort. He continued bringing me clams as he'd done when Cath was here, and from time to time I made him a stew to take home, something that would last him a few days. When he met a girl in town, Gord soon left the cabin and the dunes to start his own life out in the world somewhere.

I missed Cath when the autumn fogs rolled in, and soon found I didn't have the enthusiasm to continue on that work without her. Placing our books and tools up on the shelf, I sank down into a mood that seemed to rise over to me from the sea itself.

Why bother looking for essences, I told myself, *when no one has actually found them.? Or if they have, it doesn't mean that I will. They lived long ago and now in this age it is more difficult.* I was disheartened, feeling the pull of the undertow.

I barely continued my breathing practices each morning, ate what was leftover in the pot each day, not bothering to heat it up, and made stronger and stronger coffee.

The other Dunites were all the same, they'd felt it too. When we gathered for our autumn feast at Moy Mell it was clear to us all that something had shifted. This was one of the worst autumns we could remember. We drank to that cruel queen of the season who took our souls and squeezed them until there was little left in us of hope or happiness.

We took up card playing in the late afternoons. The big poker games at Moy Mell went on from around 4 until all hours or until the people living there kicked everyone out or until the whiskey was gone. The hard core gang started at 4 but I didn't get there till after 6. I'd have a bowl of cold stew then walk over to Moy Mell, just to see what was happening. It was always the same. It cheered me to see the light through the windows as I approached that merry cove. Gambling fever gripped everyone but with nothing to lose there was nothing to win either, so we weren't totally hooked. When someone got work on construction in town, they missed the games. Others just became fed up, or were too loaded by 4 to walk over to Moy Mell to play. The people living there tired of the fighting, so the daily games sort of petered out. But by then we had come through the worst of that terrible fall, and somehow winter didn't seem so bad that year.

I began the dreaming at that time. Serious dreaming that happened when I was asleep or sometimes when I was awake sitting still in solitude, letting my mind drift. The dreams came with messages, which I wrote down.

A special word, a letter or number, a vision of a person, a prescription for a combination of herbs. Oh I loved it, knowing I was in touch with some of the forces I'd been courting all summer with the failed experiments. Each dream gave me an essence which I notated.

When I read the notes afterwards they didn't make much sense. So I began writing poems or using symbols instead. It was as if I was keeping two sets of books, like an accountant for a crooked company. One was for me, so I could know what had actually happened, and one was for the rest of the world in case I was ever audited, I thought to myself. The set for the rest of the world was also for me too, to keep up appearances to myself. To prove to myself that I hadn't gone mad, to tell myself that everything really did make sense and was as significant as it felt.

Well it wasn't, of course, and the messages became either light or dark. Soon I had a battle of good and evil on my hands. Some days I didn't know how I was going to survive. With the dreams, daydreams, notation, translation into everyday life, I was so busy and absorbed I didn't have time for anyone else. The dark days and moons of winter rolled by.

Two pals knocked on my door. The sound knocked me out of my reverie. They looked around my once pristine cabin in shock. Now a total shambles, I saw through their eyes: it was a mess, food everywhere, piles of papers, notes and charts. On the wall I'd tacked up some pages with numbers on them linked with threads. I hadn't eaten that day either, and hadn't washed my hair or clothes for a while, so I think it might have been a bit stinky in there too, not just from the old food.

Bewildered about why they'd come, I guessed they'd been watching me for a while and decided it was time. Might have been overdue, but it wasn't too late.

I hadn't talked to anyone for a while, so at first I was rusty, but soon in a rush I told them all about the visions, the work, the new direction for knowledge and understanding, the essences, how I was so close to the answer now, and I showed them the two sets of books and my plans for the corporation based on my discoveries, all meticulously detailed and outlined with colourful illustrations. I couldn't draw but I could make shapes and forms with harmonious colours, and these abstract illustrations brought new dimensions to my document. The notes held symbols of the inexplicable and carried clues from one set of books to the more public version. I was getting them ready, you see, to be taken up to Mount Shasta any day now, so I had to keep them in top shape.

The visions had explained to me that the ascended masters were awaiting the results of my work, and would take it into the akashic record which had a library of such works deep in a secret crystal cave in Mount Shasta. Not the Mount Shasta that we see, of course, but a parallel mountain inside it that can only be accessed by the masters.

THE MERKABA

One night during that strange time, Pat had come to me, showing me how to write the letters with numbers encoded on the page, and then how to connect the numbers with thread, then to read the patterns of these connections, projecting them like acetate overlays on everything I would see or think. It was a distancing game that was quite serious. Like a vehicle of some sort, it took me far from everyday perception and consciousness. I felt less and less of the normal world. I drew the patterns of these number connections and made a small booklet of only these, so I could memorize them. In my meditations and concentrations, I traced their silver outlines over and over again in the akasha just behind my closed eyes. From time to time I'd look at the pattern and then at the world through that pattern. Soon objects in my cabin took the place of those numbers, and the connection between the objects made new patterns that were three-dimensional. If I sat in one particular place on the floor I could be in the centre of this latticework. By this time, I didn't need to use the threads to join the nodes, I could just see them in my mind's eye as lines of light. This perfect spot, I knew, was my merkaba. From here I could travel interdimensionally through time.

I saw this merkaba in other places too. A tiny one in the clusters of grasses, the stars held so many. There was the floating one that hovered in light at dawn, and there were groups of flying ones heading to the sun at sunset.

One came to me at night, glittering. Its ringing woke me from sleep. It landed in that perfect spot, the place I'd marked with a white circle on the floor. As it moved, I saw someone was inside it, a little person. It was a baby. The light lines disappeared, leaving the baby behind.

Oh oh oh oh it was my own little Susannah, my own stillborn child. Oh so many tears. She turned so I could see her innocent eyes; she was crying tears of her own. And then she spoke, directly to my mind, not with her voice. "I am all right, are you?"

"Not really," I replied.

"I'll look after you now."

Somehow she came to my feet and I picked her up, holding her in my lap as if I were a Renaissance Madonna. The baby Jesus was always proportioned more like a little grownup than an infant; she was like that, too. And wise. When she dissolved as I held her, I cried. Huge howling gulps of grief. Shaking, great heaving sounds roared through the cabin. All tears and snot and sounds. Tears I didn't know were so deep within me were pouring without stopping. My mouth was gasping for air, I could barely breathe, my nose was running, stuffing, and running again. The waves shook me. I was bereft.

This is why I'd come to the dunes. Not to seek essences, but to learn to feel my own essence, my own life's pattern.

Next morning, exhausted, my eyes puffy and my throat raw, I didn't see the lattice patterns any more. Instead I sat out, looking at the light on the sand, feeling the warm sun on my skin. The patterns were dissolved, invisible to both my mind and heart.

That day, the neighbours knocked on my door. I looked around at my cabin and saw a royal mess. I ran my hand through my matted hair and realized I hadn't brushed or washed it for weeks.

"I'd better see the doctor now." It was a Saturday afternoon, and they walked me into town.

I told him everything. My life had been going so well, I'd been working in a small store and thinking I'd go to college. Yes, I was one of those women always reading a book, curious about more than daily life. Ambitious for learning. When I met Mitch he seemed like an ordinary guy, a nice boy. There was something intriguing about him. I began to think of him night and day, coming together with him in the evenings after work and all weekend. Well, I got pregnant, and when it happened he ran the other way. He just took off and went east. I was in shock and despair. I wanted us to get married but he left before we could even talk about it. Night after night I cried myself to sleep in worry and abandonment.

When my baby came the world turned black. She didn't live to be born, she was already gone by the time I pushed her out.

Cath was my friend even back then. She'd married and had her son Aidan, but separated soon after. While I was terrified and alone and crying all the time, she brought me to live with her, to "help her out".

Somehow, telling the doctor the whole story brought some peace to my heart, and I left his place feeling that I could start again. My dune friends waited for me at the café. After coffee and fries we headed back home, first stopping at the depot to look for stray vegetables.

VITAMIN DEFICIENCY

"Vitamin deficiency." That's what the doctor in town pronounced after I'd told him what happened.

"You need more fresh vegetables, take these supplements, and walk every day. As soon as the weather warms, I want you to swim in the ocean. Walk down to the beach and jump in. Every day, at least once. You've neglected your body and your own good health. And stop the coffee. Limit it to one or two cups a day. And the drinking. Try not to have any strong drink for a month or more. You'll be surprised at how fit you'll feel. And rely on your friends, they're here to help."

I followed his simple and wise prescription for the rest of my life, adding to it the regular breathing exercises, a few of the Chinese exercises that a friend had shown me, and some basic yoga postures.

My dune neighbours took turns coming over in the mornings and helping me clean up, bringing some fresh water and food and conversation. Gradually I came back to the world a new person, and began to feel happier and more whole.

I knew in my heart that I'd gone over the edge of sanity when I'd been waiting every day for the masters to take my account to Mount Shasta's double. My logical mind had said, "this just cannot be," but it was drowned out by such convincing evidence in my inner communications that I had no choice but to comply and prepare for them, just in case. The world as I knew it had been melting before my eyes, replaced by a glittering sparking nowhere of vibrational beings.

CATH

I spent a good two years in the dunes and it was my home, my transformational furnace, my solace and my place of peace. There I became the person I am now. I faced my darkest fears, deepest self doubt, greatest ambition, and most grandiose self-glorification. I became a small person in the wide world, and a great being in the cosmic symphony. I learned to become more human. Or did I? The jury may still be out on that one. Ask my so-called friends from the past. They can't understand me now, and can't relate to much of what I say. They still invite me to the occasional event or gathering; we just aren't as close as we had been.

But my relationship with Cath hasn't shifted. After she left Gord to his year out in the dunes before college, she changed quite a bit but the compass remained true. Her time in the dunes caused her to open even more fully to her own life's purpose.

One night when we sat outside with a beach fire, talking about our lives, she shared some of what had happened between her and Derek. I knew it had been a bad relationship, especially close to the end. She told me she'd locked herself in the bathroom while he'd raged outside the door, calling her every name in the book. In tears she waited until he stopped and she heard the car start. Fearful that he might have taken Aidan with him, she rushed into the bedroom to check. No. At least that, she thought. This had been the last straw, he was getting worse.

Instead of just making sniping comments about her appearance or how she was doing things, she found him always angry and irritable about the world in general. No one was treating him right, the way he deserved, and they were often rude and insulting. He spent evenings after work brooding and thinking about the problems of the day, and not speaking to her particularly. Well Cath was a young woman then, with her life ahead of her. Their son was a sweet and gentle baby, and it should have been a time of happiness and promise. Instead, Derek was always in a turmoil about one thing or another, and she spent every dinnertime listening to his list of problems caused by others who weren't right, weren't good, weren't whatever they should be. Then after dinner he brooded till bedtime.

Cath had to be careful that Aidan didn't make a peep, a difficult and impossible task with a small baby. So she took to coming over to my place with the baby several evenings a week. I needed company so much and we really had fun, laughing and chatting until 9:30 pm, when she started looking at the clock and rushing home before Derek became angry, wondering where she was.

She could hear him saying, "Where were you? I don't like my schedule to be upset, it makes my sleep uneven and you know I need my sleep."

"Oh sorry dear, I didn't keep track of the time. I'll make it better next time. At least you got some time to yourself. I know you like the peace and quiet."

He was standing at the door one night when she came home. Just blocking the door and laughing in a taunting way, not letting her pass. With the baby in one arm, the baby bag and her purse in the other, she moved from left to right trying to get by.

"Come on Derek, let me get by," she said.

"That's what you get for going out," he sneered, "It gets harder and harder to get back in." He laughed at his game.

It was a standoff. He would not let her pass and she would not stop trying. Aidan started crying louder and louder. One of the neighbours next door came out to walk her dog for the night and asked if they needed any help.

"Oh no," Cath said brightly, "We're just fooling around. We didn't mean to disturb you."

The neighbour'd seen this before, and raised her eyebrows before walking on. Cath glared at Derek and he let her pass, giving her a little shove when she went by. She rushed Aidan upstairs to the changing table, her hands shaking as she mechanically took off his little sweater and hat, and changed and fed him, putting her sleeping sweet boy to bed for the night (or as much of the night as he would allow until he woke crying for more.) Now it was Cath who was crying. She didn't want Derek to know, so she went immediately to bed, calling goodnight down to him.

"You're going to bed pretty early," he said.

"I know, there's lots to do tomorrow, remember?"

Cath told more stories about her early life with Derek. It sounded like a nightmare to me. I came to see why she spent so much time with me, and not with other married women with kids. It was just too sad for her. She couldn't share their experiences and there was no way she could have a social life with them and their families.

She met and talked with other young mums at the park or the play group or library. They planned to meet again the next day, but then it started. The invitations to dinner or Saturday afternoon visits with the families. She had dreaded that next step in the social game. Derek insisted that no one come to their home unless he approved them, and since he didn't approve of anyone, that was that. And of course he refused to go to anyone's home for dinner either. They tried it once but it was a disaster. Not only was she unprepared for what he said to people at the table, she wasn't in any position after that to return the invitation. Not that they would have come anyways. And for two weeks after any event, he went over and over the conversations, what she should have said, should have worn, should have done. How she should have supported him when he made his comments about the dinner, or sarcastically belittled their interests. Nothing was ever right or good enough. She was in despair.

"If it hadn't been for Aidan I don't know what I would have done."

"I knew Derek was unhappy too," she said, "But I didn't realize the extent of it. Plus I was young, so I didn't have experience with people. I certainly didn't know anything about men in those days."

After he lost his job, he spent the days at home. Cath had no freedom at all, and he began to tell her how to look after Aidan and how to regulate his feeding, all kinds of scientific correct advice based on his own ideas and his need for quiet. Aidan was put outside in his carriage, to take in the fresh air on the porch as he slept. Sometimes the baby was left to cry there. One winter day when Cath went to the store, she came back to find him sobbing his heart out. Derek kept the windows closed to keep the heat in and save on the bill and hadn't known he was crying. Or so he said. Cath didn't quite believe him, because when she was in the living room, she could hear through the glass.

"That's the mother's special hearing, not mine," Derek had said.

As things went from bad to worse, Cath started to plan her escape. That's how she thought of it, as an escape. Her sister lived not too far from her, so she arranged a plan to take just a few things over to her sister's each time she went there. Not much, because Derek was pretty watchful about what she took with her. Once he asked, "Why are you taking that big winter coat over there?"

"Oh Sue wants to make one just like it," she lied, "So she's using this for a pattern."

Cath went back to work, and arranged for Sue to look after Aidan in the day.

"It'll be easier for you," she told Derek, "And Sue's lonely these days, now her kids are all in school." Derek looked after all the money, so her pay went straight to the bank account, but she knew she'd still have the job once she left.

Her opportunity came when Derek went to his mother's place for a few days, to help with her storm windows and fall yard work. Cath just left everything. Didn't look back. Went to Sue's, then called him at his mother's, to tell him, because she felt bad that when he got home no one would be there.

He took it quietly, then laughed in a weird way. He told her she was a stupid cunt, a bitch who didn't have a clue. He wasn't at his mother's place, he was with Loreen, and he was the one who was leaving, not her. She could go fuck herself for all he cared.

And telling me this, at the fireside, Cath cried and cried while I held her, gently wiping her hair from her forehead. She'd always told the story the way she'd wanted it to be. She'd planned her escape, left him, and then later on he had taken up with Loreen. On the rebound.

This was a sadness she'd carried with her all that time, and she hadn't had any man in her life since then. I was afraid of any man getting too close too. We had that in common.

There is a truth serum that comes over us all in the dunes: there is no way to survive unless we become true to ourselves.

NOTATION AND THE ESSENCES, BACKGROUND ON THE ESSENCE ATELIER
COURSE

Before the dunes, Cath and I were delighted to discover that the Essence
Atelier offered open classes. We signed up right away for the introductory
evening sessions.

She was interested in aromatherapy, while I had my sights set on
discovering nothing less than the essence of all things, or something to that
effect. I needed a place to go that wasn't work, and this one class a week was
a welcome diversion and inspiration.

It had been a while since the baby, and I'd put all that behind me. I'd gone
back to work part-time, but I was without any direction, just in a holding
pattern. Cath was lucky that her nephew, Gordie, was able to babysit for her
on class nights.

The sessions were catalytic. Inspired, we dove right in. Seriously. We bought
all kinds of equipment and set up in her basement to do the experiments.

We'd wondered what the teacher would be like. I'd seen photos. We knew
he loved to play the violin beside rushing water in the woods. He had flowing
white hair and a van dyke beard, extremely well-groomed.

"The flood of negative ions produced by the stream mingles with the fine
vibrations of the sound waves from the violin," he explained. "This creates a
profound exhilarating experience, which varies depending on the place, the
time of day, and the season. These variations themselves are a kind of music,
only not "heard." Known in this way, each experience plays as a note in this
larger musical piece."

He said that greater music can be known in overview, and by condensing
time-space it would be possible to hear it.

"How can I do that?" I wondered.

He enjoyed playing at sunrise and sunset. Noon was too strong for him, the
finer ions were not in play as the sun flattened everything. 4 pm was the ideal
time for so many actions, as was 4 am for others. And so forth. My notebooks
were filled. He recommended books by others, yoga books on swaradaya and
books from antiquity. Cath began her serious library right then, sourcing old
books and ordering them. When the books came, we pored over the volumes
together, and eagerly learned what we could from them about the nature of
this work.

Together, Cath and I studied books on the essences in particular. We began hunting for the perfect notation system for the essences, one uniquely suited to today's requirements. From various "Books of Secrets", we saw the work of the earlier seekers, written in longhand and often in codes known only to them and their pupils. Some relied heavily on illustrations to convey the meaning. With signs and symbols for the main substances, time of day, season, weather and other conditions at the time of the extraction, these symbols gave condensed and essential information to the next seeker.

Some began using mathematical or algebraic formulas, others combined these with symbols and visionary illustrations. Soon an elaborate system built up. This was completely incomprehensible to anyone who didn't understand the systems used for the communications. The neophyte seeker had to learn these languages before beginning to study the works of the past, and that was another serious barrier to entry. A student could end up never touching the materials at all, only learning the language.

Not only did students need to learn these codes, they needed the leisure time in which to dedicate themselves to this study. Only then could they begin to set up for themselves. We had heard there was still a strong apprenticeship system in place, where mentors taught novices in their workshops. Hands on. We didn't know how to contact the independents working solo. They were esoteric, hidden.

But we did understand that each mentor was also learning, for there were no grandmasters left alive if ever there were grandmasters. We speculated: perhaps they were present but hiding in plain sight, as mentors. We couldn't know.

"There are very few," our teacher said, "who truly understand the essences today. In this age of materialism we are fixated on the physical, and on making everything a physical process. Many of the finer processes are not physical at all, but they are not religious or meditative either."

He often told us, "It is a mountain to be climbed, and a secret cave to be entered."

We were entranced. Here we met the others. Some had been involved for five years now.

We formed a group outside of class, and met every weekend we could, also some weeknights.

Cath had to stay home because of Aidan, so we met at her place in the evenings. Some Saturdays he was with his dad and his stepmother, so Cath was free for some weekend overnights.

Not much happened at first. Then one night something shifted. We were working with the materials in the basement lab, as usual.

Cath said, "Did you feel that?"

Mike jumped up, "What the hell?"

A small ball of light went through the room at eye level. It's true. I saw it, and so did the others. We all saw it and felt it.

How it happened was a mystery. We notated it and repeated our actions leading up to the event. We tried for several weeks, then realized it was unrepeatable.

"We should try to do it again next year at the same time. That might repeat it."

"But don't you see, the conditions won't be the same as that night, not ever."

"Even if the room was the same, which it would not be, we ourselves would be different."

"It's true. Plus, the weather could be different, all conditions would not be exact, so it is not repeatable at all."

"How could we even select the date? What calendar would we be using?" and so on we discussed all the variables.

"So then how can we prove it, or learn from it?

"I don't see what the point is of writing it up and trying to repeat it, when everything is always changing, different and infinitely unrepeatable."

"I don't know but it seems to be within us to try. Part of the whole process somehow."

"At least we can look at the account and remember how it happened."

"Maybe the writing gives another iteration of the experience, one that can be shared and discussed?"

"Or writing it down can hold some of the essence of the time and place?"

"I think we're on to something. By notating, we can hold the essence of the time and place long enough for other minds to tune into it."

"And keep it as an essence for even longer thanks to their concentration on it."

"It can also be a sort of time travel in a way, led by the thoughts held in words."

"I think it's in the sharing. Repeating it in the sharing can actually convey some of the message. Maybe even another aspect to the unfoldment can only come when it's shared."

"True. Well, we've seen it and others could at least know it's possible, or know something is possible, outside of what we imagine can be."

"That's what I feel we're going toward, and I hope you're with me on this. We aren't making things permanent by writing them down, but they do become lasting."

"I think I get it. This is a way experience hooks into the larger system of thought and awareness. It goes beyond the instinctual and into the realms of ideas."

"And further...to shared ideas."

"That's the other part of this: we share the same perception when the writing can convey it, not in the words but in the reference to the experience."

"Just in the same way a surveyor makes a map!" I said.

Imagine my surprise later, when the first thing I found when I went into the cabin in the dunes was the surveyor's notebook.

"Take one year away," I was told in a vivid dream when studying at the Atelier, "And you will do the work that would take you ten years part-time."

The dream really was to come true, when I set out to the dunes, but by then I had moved far away from the Essence Atelier.

THE ESSENCE ATELIER

The hidden harmonies began to show themselves not just in thought and perception but also in everyday life.

A friend used to pray "disclose to us thy divine light, which is hidden in our souls, that we may know and understand life better." Everything was happening just like that. The hidden light of the soul began to reveal itself more and more. Life seemed to open up and show itself, like the mountain cave in the fairy tale of *Open Sesame*, revealing treasures.

For me, the treasures were not gold or silver, just clear dreams and thoughts or memories. Seeing my life from another point of view, events looked entirely different from a new angle. I needed to let down the shield of my everyday way of seeing. Then I began to intuit the forces and influences in the events of my life up until now. I felt permission to relax. Guided by unseen karmic patterns, I could have done nothing other than what I did. Now that I could see some of these patterns, it was up to me to stop or transform them, with the help of the hidden harmonies.

Seeking the essences was my way of discovering these event-creating influences. Some of these influences threatened my life or the lives of those I loved. I don't mean only illnesses or accidents, but also other human beings who wished me harm. Well, not me, actually, just anyone who got in their way or who could be used or turned for nefarious purposes.

They called the teacher at the Essence Atelier "Master Nikolai". Some said he was using the students in his school to amass a power base that he could use to grow into a powerful magician. This was just nonsense. Those of us who knew him could tell how wrong they were. He was sweet and gentle, and was adept at collecting the finest essences, particularly dews. His one devoted student, Marie Claire, was his lifelong companion. She was his chronicler, and had been dutifully creating his notations in the book they called *The Illumination of All Life*. Here was set out his work from the early days 40 years past, up to the present day, handwritten in well-loved volumes, preserved for future pupils.

For the classes, Marie Claire had given us all copies of the charts of correspondences: the harmonies between substances, weather, place, time and stars, as well as moon phases and astrology. They used astrology and mathematics as basic sciences, with the structure of chemistry built upon them, and an addition of what they called "The Sentimental Attributes" which were our human qualities and emotions. There was much more to it than that, of course, but we were beginners. There was no indication that we could use breath, for example, or that we could change weather, heal others or predict the future.

One grid showed days of the week, corresponding colours and their effects. Our assignment was to wear the colour of the element of that day, with an attunement to the events of the day in relation to that element, then in the evening to light a candle of that colour and write our account. We were to define one emotion or feeling that could describe the day, and write it in our diary. Weekends were free and exempt from class requirements, but soon the group of us got together, compared notes and asked for extra guidance.

After a few months we'd also learned to read the influence of the moon in our affairs. Adding the lunar overlay to our days meant we were on a ship that moved with the tides, and we were no longer stuck plodding along on land. As you can imagine, travelling the entire zodiac for a full year was also a wonderful area of study, relating to place, time and season. Each of us had differing experiences and harmonic correspondences because of the variance in our place and time of birth.

We knew that Master Nikolai was using our charts and research to help him in his compilation of *The Illumination of All Life*. We were fine with it, happy to take part in such a noble effort. Only one of us had concerns but he'd been the skeptic in the group from the beginning. He told us that Master Nikolai and Marie Claire went over our weekly assignments on the weekends so they could manipulate and hypnotize us, then when we came to class on Thursday we were more malleable and willing to do as he asked. He said that Nikolai and Marie Claire were feeding off our subtle energies and we would soon discover what they were up to. Why was he there at all, if this is the kind of stuff he was thinking? We all knew that trust is one of the foundations of this work.

One evening we were lined up at the end of class. Marie Claire brought us forward one at a time, and Nikolai placed a mark on each of us: on the arm or the ankle or wrist, depending on our correspondence charts. It was a small emblem or glyph of some sort. He painted it on us using a mixture of herbs and reddish oil.

"This will increase your sensitivity for the week to come," Marie Claire told us. "Particularly at the full moon this Saturday. From 4 pm to 3 am be aware. You may notice something more…"

Saturday at four o'clock we gathered, and didn't notice a thing. Finally I went home to bed. I dreamed that Nikolai lined us up and each glyph was part of a magical alphabet, spelling one word, one magic word of power that he could read. I couldn't make sense of it though. At one point in the dream, we were all touching one another: ankle to shoulder to wrist to calf, wherever the glyphs were we made them join by touching, like a game of twister but all together. Of course our arms and legs couldn't actually reach that way, but in the dream they extended and connected. Then we stood in a circle, facing inward. Nikolai and Marie Claire were in the centre. I suddenly realized, "Oh my god, this is some kind of sex rite." Frozen in place, shocked, I stared forward.

Above our heads the glyphs shone like diadems. They were spelling something I didn't understand. Naked except for the marks, we stood watching Nikolai and Marie Claire. They were on fire in the centre of our circle. A clear high-pitched tone filled the room with a piercing resonance. I was submerged in waves of energy. In a flash it seemed we were all on fire, adoring the life force in its greatest essence. Consumed with desire for glorious explosion into the abyss, I woke in the spasms of an intense orgasm. I felt weak and confused for three days afterwards.

I broached the subject of the dream with the others, and they'd had dreams too. One was on a journey, another was...well they were all different. And we were all weak afterwards. All our dreams included the glyphs, the diadems, a ritual of passion that ended in the same way: waking in an unexplained orgasm. Some thought it was a purge of some kind, others a possession, others an opening or ritual of power.

Next class, radiant and filled with joy, Marie Claire looked ten years younger. She thanked us for taking part in their full moon ritual. I was shocked to hear her talk this way, as if it had actually happened. Did this mean she was aware of my dream? Oh God, I was shocked and ashamed, I looked around the class and others were blushing or looking downward.

"There is no need for shame," she said, "We all have the generative power. Open to it and learn to live freely in life's greatest joy on earth. Never fear it. Only learn to use it wisely. Find your sacred partner and make a beautiful experience for him or her. It is your birthright to be happy, but do not abuse it. Now you have had the experience, you can go into life with more understanding. It is not good to close away the strength of this world and let yourself become cold and dry. Never lose your love of life and its joys. Even the carnal pleasures have been given for your happiness and the expansion of all life. Now go and give this to others, and accept nothing less for yourself, either. What we gave you was a demonstration, do not repeat it.

"You will find now that when you imagine or recall this, all you will see are the glyphs above your heads. Together they spell the words that mean 'We worship all life at the root of this world. We offer our adoration to God all that is divine. Accept my sacrifice.' There will be no further feeling, for it is now complete. You have received the essence."

I looked around at the others, uncomfortable. I felt I'd been used, almost like a rape. My energy had been taken against my will to feed their personal power. No matter what her words were, I felt too numb to be disturbed, still in a state of shock. It was too much, too soon.

I had to leave the Essence Atelier. This was not a direction I wanted to follow. I called Cath and we talked for hours. That night I broke down and sobbed for all I had lost: the baby, the perfunctory sex that had got me pregnant in the first place, the birth experience, my dear dead baby. I saw now that it was as if it had all happened without me. Then I understood that I was being healed, but in a way I'd never expected. I intuited the next step was for me to act, not to think or dream.

The next night Mike called and I asked him over, taking our conversation toward the full moon and dream. Sure enough, he'd had a similar dream. We went toward each other with a true loving intention. Soon we were in bed together in an embrace that took me far from earth and high into the heavens. "All the doors opened themselves, all the lamps lighted themselves." We were loving and living in love, the next many days were a continuity of this bliss and blessing from the Lord of Life. Soon the memories and shame of the hypnosis spell in the dream were replaced by the greater reality of our connection. We had initiated one another and healed each other.

We knew it was temporary, and wouldn't last forever. Soon we were thrust into other more challenging conditions. I'd left the group by then, and it further broke apart when the class series came to an end. Mike's father became ill, so he went back home to care for him. "I'd regret it for the rest of my life if I didn't go back and help him now," he told me. Mike's new sensitivity had shown him how to give of himself, to love and engage.

I soon learned to do things one at a time, and to see them in their simplicity. It was a practice that enriched every part of my life. I left the Essence Atelier far behind me and set out to "know and understand life better."

In particular I needed to find a balance, so I went to the gym and went walking every day to keep my left and right sides balanced. I also did the alternate nostril breathing, having learned it from a yoga book. It dawned on me that I had learned a great deal from everyone there, each had given me a gift of some sort. I make a list of people and their gifts.

And what had I done for them?

This, and who am I? and why am I here? were burning questions that I was now in the process of answering. Yet the process, I discovered, had only just begun. I soon was taken down to the empty place again. After only three weeks, I stopped entirely. I was no longer doing much of anything, and had no energy for walking, or even reading or thinking.

DREAM KEY

I found that life in the dunes was so much a world in itself, that instead of being on retreat, I was actually just trading one world for another. My new life did have more time for stillness, and an open vibration allowing more experience to occur in the inner side of life.

I was so happy to find a way to live simply in the presence of the divine, and to find my own way in my inner chambers. Up the spiral staircase, to the place in the attic where roses bloom in the fireplace and the lady of the house offers magical tea most ceremoniously. Here we sing songs that evolve from the simplest of chants into harmonies of exquisite complexity.

In the dunes, I imagined she was my particular grandmother, whose workshop and notebooks were magical to my mind's eye. Wishing this could be a world I, too, could enter, I saw her studio at the top of the stairs as a place where the cosmic forces mingled with those of earth.

I dreamed at night that these worlds were self-sustaining, fed by pure streams that revealed themselves when I looked at them, then hid themselves back into the dull everyday when they no longer held my attention.

I dreamed again and again of places in nature where I would look at anything at all and it would open up its secret.

A tree told me its name and it wasn't a name in any language I could know, or write.

A path showed me its underside, where I saw all the footprints of everyone who had walked that path, humans and animals, and starlight also passing over it, to create a moire of amazing beauty revealing the lines of light as a living three-dimensional patterning.

A stream sang its songs as I sat on the rocks, and when the sun hit the water, the song soared into heights of adoration, and when a cloud covered the sun, it hummed deeper melodies that would wrench the heart.

I felt something was speaking to me, and there was a message for me that nature wanted me to know, and tell to others.

In thought, the lady who was a grandmother told me this: "You must promise me that you will write your own *Book of Secrets*, and that you will not copy from any other volumes to do so. You can use them as inspiration of course. A true *Book of Secrets* is always written directly by the author, and describes only experiments and events as seen and known, never copied from another. Can you do this?"

"Yes," I replied solemnly, also in thought, and with true intent. "When do I start?"

"You begin when you are ready, after your faith in the world has been shattered, and when you receive the coming dream."

In the following days of my deepest despair I dreamed nightly of large plants and rainforests, of natural rock formations shining in moonlight. Unrecognizable faces appeared through the foliage, or as if carved on the rocks, some human, some animal, some like spirits not seen on earth except in dream or vision.

Night after night such dreams processed my feelings. A baby was found in the forest, with leaves sheltering it from the rain. Once a floating basket made of flowers and vines held a baby floating downstream. The baby was always asleep. Once there was a baby in a nest high in the tree canopy, moving in the wind, almost falling but not falling. Still the baby slept. The baby was never to be born.

"I will never come to you," her voice said to me, "never in this life or in this way. The world is too hard, too harsh for my soul and spirit. I will not sacrifice myself this way. It is not your decision. I know you love me, I know you wanted only to be my mother. It was never to happen, I could not allow it. Haven't you read Blake's *Book of Thel*? I am here for you and you alone, my incarnation was always incomplete and will remain dormant until the world is refined again, as it was in the golden age." This voice came into my mind from the baby's mind as I dreamed. Even in the dream I wondered if I was imagining it all, and if I was really off the deep end.

In another dream, a grandmother came to see me at my parents' house. Knocking on the door of my room, then opening the door to see me lying in bed under the quilt, facing the wall. It was 4 o'clock in the afternoon.

"Hello, pumpkin," she said softly.

I turned over, not believing my eyes. "You came all this way to see me!?"

"How are you, sweetheart?"

"Terrible, I guess. But getting through."

"Tell me …"

And so I did, I told her everything, in tears for the first time in weeks, and using up all the kleenex from the big snotty globby crying that heaved through me as she held me.

"Yes, yes, yes...." she said, "I know , I know," as she wiped my hair from my face.

Then she gave me a small key. "This is the key to my studio file cabinet. Here you will find my volumes. Have you had the dream yet?"

I'd forgotten. "The dream?" I murmured.

The next night I saw the one with the golden hands. Innumerable golden hands, each doing something different, and each with an eye in the palm. I looked into the eye in one of the golden hands. It became a mouth and spoke. Its mouth opened slowly but I didn't hear what it said at first.

"Now," it said to me. "Now." Then the hands all moved together creating waves like an ocean of gold. I heard the reverberating word *Now* and woke to a loud cracking sound.

72

GREAT ESSENCE: THE CRY OF THE HEART

I feel the cry of my bursting heart, filled to breaking with the world's woes, and as the song goes: "Sometimes it's best to let it, who could regret such exquisite hurt?"

My whole body shakes and weeps with the pains and sorrows. I sit by the fireside and send into the wholehearted flames all this twisted sadness, this immense pressure from the charge. The charge breaks through finally and without impediment: the supreme electric charge that has been incubating the last several months, since it was first invoked.

My head moves from side to side, turning from one shoulder to the other, from left to heart to right to above and down into the heart again only to return to the left, down again to the heart, over to the right, then above, and down piercing the heart once more. With each rotation of this spiral the energies rise and return, rise and return. Soon a vortex is created where the energy rises, while from above a divine response enters in turn.

When my own third eye beams its laser into my heart, then circles upward before descending again, it is a profound self-sacrifice of illumination. In this action, the divine reality pierces itself into the compassionate manifestation so only love may exist, nothing else. All is this love.

The trunk of a tree is wound round and round by a spiral vine. When sunlight catches it just so, a flame rises in the fire, as if to say we are all reaching upward to you dear one, so we make a leap even higher. Flame to sun.

Repetition and revolution show spiral patterns of the evolving goddess, who winds around all that may grow to fullness. We who are on the rotating earth, circling the great comet that is our sun, dragging with it the planet family of our little world that we call the universe; we now stand as if perfectly still, as if we were statues with arms outstretched, and around us the butterflies of souls and consciousness, the flowers and birds of awakening, and all the manifestations that ever could be, fly around us in never-ending joyful bliss.

I dug deep and threw up. I held my stomach and groaned while I gave birth to the transpersonal monsters conceived in human history of incest, rape and violence. I am not in denial of all the dark and twisted knots, the roots of dead trees, the skulls and dried blood, the wily ways of the desires that are always finding a place to infest and multiply within. I've seen and felt the cold and damp, the cruel and sharp. Because of this I am planting small powerful seeds of care and compassion. They grow naturally for they are native to this soil, and they need little light and water for they are most hardy.

Take some. They were a gift of the Green One who appears suddenly, and, as mysteriously, leaves. Let us plant again the ancient garden, even if this world is given over to the bulls as Rumi said. If the bulls trample it we will plant another. If the bulls pave the land, we will find new land. If the bulls stop us there too, we will find a way, even if it means dying that our bodies may provide fertile ground for the seeds of the new life.

Tears may be behind my eyes but now there is peace within me.

This essence is a seed, to be planted in the human heart.

Attar 2

FROM MOY MELL TO CHITTAKASH

The Lake Isle of Innisfree by W.B. Yeats

I will arise and go now, and go to Innisfree,
And a small cabin build there, of clay and wattles made;
Nine bean rows will I have there, a hive for the honey bee,
And live alone in the bee loud glade.

And I shall have some peace there, for peace comes dropping slow,
Dropping from the veils of the morning to where the cricket sings;
There midnight's all a glimmer, and noon a purple glow,
And evening full of the linnet's wings.

I will arise and go now, for always night and day
I hear lake water lapping with low sounds by the shore;
While I stand on the roadway, or on the pavements grey,
I hear it in the deep heart's core.

Moy Mell is my Innisfree.

Journey Behind the Seeming

At the cabin in the dunes, lamps are lit inside as the sun sets. One by one the stars come out to meet their vortexes of energies in the coves, to play the waves, to send their beams down upon us in the patterns we know as life's events.

And here we feel the wheel of time and change, the seasonal wheel that reveals at each turn.

Inside myself I ask, "How do I find the dark matter behind this wheel of change? Isn't this where all the condensed compression happens?"

I think about what I know or sense about the compression of charcoal to diamond: that is according to the law of the wheel. But the compression further to a diamond essence? That is almost the reverse of itself, it must happen in the dark. Just as day turns into night, what is seen has as its counterpart that which is unseen. And what is known has what is unknown behind it.

So with Moy Mell. It exists as a stage set or a toy world, behind which the dark night, like a fog, engulfs the tiny lantern-light showing in the window. Inside real poets laugh and play, declaim and sing, argue and discover. This evening, for example, tentacles of darkness, sensitively probing, find their way into the cracks in the cabin, into the minds of the men and women who are laughing together. More than most places, Moy Mell has openings for these probes, and more than most people, the poets are sensitive to the probings of their minds. Their hearts are open because they cannot help themselves, and so the probes enter there first. Melancholy is a natural outcome of these darker probings, but those who learn to understand their meaning find ways to live with this.

These probes and darknesses are not separate from us. They are part of our condition and, moreover, part of what we are here to learn and live within. We can make it ours and understand it. Pulling from the darkness into the light we are working the powers of the human heart.

We become even more alive when these challenges appear in the forms they do. They seem to come simply from chittakash, which is the place where we enact the scenes of life in the mind's eye.

My own mind's eye opened early and it has been functioning as a warning to me ever since. I must never look back, only forward. Behind is that blackness I told you of. Can the whole person see herself from before and behind at the same time? I'm asking a question inside my own mind, and hear the answer, "Yes we will try to go into this new way of living, with the balance of dark and light."

It's an answer that doesn't make sense to me, and I feel that someone unseen might be here with me, so I ask aloud, "Who's speaking here and why should I even try to listen? I'm here to experience the land of the heart, the landscape of beauty and light. Why then should I even consider or contend with these dark figures who hold inexplicable notebooks and show glyphs of complexities, horrors and torturous conditions?"

"Because you will never be whole unless you dare to see even this." It was the wise one who replied. "There are two dark portals, they look like simple archways, like cave openings. Inside these you see what the world is all about. Do you dare to enter them?"

"But why are there two? Isn't one enough?"

"You must choose which door you enter. The left door shows one path, the right another. For the way is forked, and you can only choose one way here."

"I don't understand why I must choose. Who set this up? It doesn't seem fair to me either, when there is no way to reverse my steps and come out to the other doorway."

"Go in and see for yourself."

The arched and smoky gateway wasn't a door but a kind of weird threshold. I stepped over it. I'd gone to the left. I felt the right one would be normal so I wanted something else. The minor key, the left side. The moon, the gentle, the receptive, the woman. Or so I thought, as I stepped closer to the door. It had a power that interested me, but I couldn't say why. Grey, smoky violet haze and fog. I could see nothing. It wasn't dark and it wasn't light, it was nothing. Darkly cloudy I guess.

I remained there. It was a little damp.

"Hmm." I thought, "I'm no Dante exploring the underworld here. I'm just a person looking to understand something that is not so easily known. Maybe this is the fog of unknowing?"

I thought of all the other references made by the mystics about that stage of development. But the longer I remained there, the foggier my own mind became. Soon I felt as if my head was full of cotton batting. My eyes seeing little or nothing but this fog, my ears hearing nothing at all but a sort of white noise. With nothing to touch, taste or smell, I soon fell into a most odd state. I think I may have been standing or walking, but could hardly tell if any part of me was moving, or even alive. At that thought I looked down and saw something below me that looked like it could have been my body. But it was just a shell. Collapsed. There was no light but I could see it anyway, and wondered if I had some sort of eyes.

"Welcome to chittakash," the voice boomed. "It was an empty space but now you are here to fill it. Your simple presence is already transforming it from nothing to something, from nowhere to somewhere. In return, it will transform you from somebody into nobody."

The voice retreated. I was left inside, looking out upon a newborn landscape of the soul. In the distance, clusters of grapes...no, not grapes but groups of souls, unborn babies together in a tight formation of bubbles or round eggs. To the south were waving flags, pennants of all colours on tall sticks fixed into the ground. To the west was a doorway. I went in immediately. It seemed urgent to me to go there.

Why I can't say. It was empty there also, but as soon as I looked around, my eyebeams created world upon world. It was so much fun to look and then see whatever I had projected, almost beyond my mind to keep up with. I couldn't calculate it all, and would never remember any of it when I got back. If I returned. And at that thought I sat down, in a frozen despair. Tears filled oceans and rained for weeks, the stars unveiled their secrets to the sea but I could only weakly observe, and had no sense of delight or wonder at this.

For my mind had become clogged with the strength of despair. I didn't want any of this anymore.

I didn't see when someone came into the chamber and lifted me out onto the sand near my cabin door. At least that's what I think happened. When I woke it was early dawn.

BOOKS OF SECRETS

The tradition of the *Book of Secrets* was based on idiosyncrasies and anecdotal methods, with recipes or prescriptions on the side for those who wished to try some of the observations for themselves.

I hesitate to refer to their procedures as experiments because they were not at all scientific. They were not repeatable and results varied widely from practitioner to practitioner. Notes such as these were simply given from adept to adept as documentation of the way of this work, and to act as an encouragement from those who had gone before.

I know that many of these were in fact bogus reports. Some copied from the works of others, some all fabrication and fantasy. The books I was looking at were in many ways fictions. Yet they weren't novels, unless you thought the writer was the protagonist. Their content wandered nowhere at all, and they soon were left almost like cookbooks, to be read and collected unused.

THE SKIRT OF THE LADY

In a dream I see my own *Book of Secrets* set with interlays that hide and show in turn the image of nature. I see this as I sit writing unreadable glyphs, sending out my dedication to the Lady, Goddess of minstrels. Those bards used to think she was the Virgin Mary, or the queen of the court at which they sang, but she was far older than that, and more pervasive. I am shown that she is none other than the earth herself, our mother Nature, the goddess who is our womb and tomb. She is more than earth, for she is Sophia, wisdom, truth lived in life. As I dedicate this *Secret* work to her, I offer my pen, my heart and being to her. I ask that I be her voice, that I be her sitting with a pen in my hand and a heart that beats just a little bit too rapidly.

I find before me a leafless tree whose bare branches bisect the space. At random angles, branches meet to portion out the view as if it were a leaded-glass window. These freeform glassless panes are triangles, rhomboids, all variant; some lines thick, others tiny and thin. My *Book of Secrets* with its episodes and portions fits perfectly into the spaces created by the tree's intersecting branches. I slot a chapter here, a section there, some larger and expanded, some small, merely stubs of the ideas they are to become. All at once I see it as a cohesive picture.

These are not random shards. The parts are not in symmetry; there is no central shape. The forms jut out to extend every which way. Yet they are whole and fit into this tree perfectly.

The lines of the tree that hold the shapes in space are like the lines of my palm that look like tributaries, creeks, rivers and streams seen from high above. The spaces between the lines of my palm are like the spaces created between the branches of this tree. Between the hand and the tree is a harmonious correspondence, one single code in the landscape terrain of rivers and creeks.

In the dream, I see that the points where the branches meet find correspondence in the stars, and in our neurons. Interdimensional orchestration produces this work, a work that exactly fits into the spaces. Each episode is framed by branches thick or thin. Nodes where the branches seem to meet join parts with all the others, some as pinpoints, some as ganglia, in poignant wabi sabi. This *Book of Secrets* is made of shards of broken mirror put back together as a naturally-formed mosaic.

It is the Lady who stands before me. The skirt of her dress is this tree. The rest of her expands, laughing above as invisible sky.

HOUSEKEEPING WITH THE SIMPLES

I had to start catching up with the housekeeping. I hadn't put the notes in order, and they were becoming unwieldy. Taking a step back, I went over all my old papers and put them into alphabetical folders. Here's where I noticed that I'd somehow overlooked the simples. I realized I was trying to leap ahead before they were truly sorted. So I listed them in the order in which they had appeared to me, and made an accurate catalogue of attributes. It took days to organize all this, but the task was very pleasant.

In remembering the simples I recalled the shape and feeling of each of them. Their scent, their shape, their colour and light, texture, taste, all had play. I noted where I had found them and how they had come to me, for it was all part of the experiential evidence that I was gathering for the collection of essences.

What is the difference between the simple and the essence? This and other questions naturally arose as I worked on the papers. Now that I had a little experience, I found that my earlier notes weren't as relevant as they'd seemed at the time. Others which had made little sense at the writing now seemed prescient and more valuable as areas of experimentation for the future.

In a separate book, I began to write out ideas for future experiments. I speculated how it would play out if I were to devote myself entirely to this task for six months or more. Not exactly sure how to do that, I continued writing and listing. Knowing that what I was creating was a crucible of my own transformation and becoming, I went forward with the task at hand.

My book fell into the category of Secret accounts as another *Book of Secrets*, or *Book of Knowledge*.

Others I'd found were fascinating but so idiosyncratic, anecdotal and unscientific, I couldn't believe they had ever been used as the basis of chemistry. But here is where the Arab scholars came in with their wisdom and alchemy. Methodical identification took the place of myth-making from old wives tales. Or did it? I had the feeling that there was also a great tradition of the simples and elements that was based on folklore and epic tales. And what is the difference between a teaching story and a fairy tale? Is it in the teller or in the listener? A fairy tale told to a child may later reveal itself to be a teaching story. I didn't want to make judgments or leaps into irrationality. I only knew that the lines move according to the wave of the times.

My exploration of the essences started me on a path of internal self-recognition. I discovered the workings of the essences in my own being: in my health and outlook, moral feelings, and so forth. It was a kind of mystical psychology, based in the traditions of the ancients, and it allowed for influences from the forces beyond my ability to see or assess.

I began to sense a next step in the work on collection of essences. The Arabs referred to this when they listed the 99 Names of God. The Chinese also did their own version with the *I Ching*, which works more in combinations rather than as single essences. I added them to my list of research study, each to be examined more carefully.

The 99 Names are tremendous essences that are great aspects that we can see at work in humanity, and in circumstances. There is much to aspire to when working in this system. A person can be enfolded in the magical multicoloured robes of divine attributes simply by speaking these names, in a particular order with a particular number, and so forth, and for a set period of time, preferably the same time each day.

How this works is an esoteric magic. The forces or aspects of being or attributes of God begin to settle there, in that holy spot consecrated to the recitation of these holy names. The circuits within the body and in the place itself begin to entrain in a rather exquisite entanglement with the invoked forces. Soon the person who has recited these words or done these works becomes more and more like that which has been called forth. It comes from both within the person and from outside...or what seems to be outside. For what really is outside any of us? We are not limited by the containment of our skin, and our bodies extend forever in finer and finer resonant waves. Not to mention thought, which is even more expansive.

Both thought and expression penetrate all worlds and exist in all times simultaneously. But this is not the goal. I'm instead looking to come into a true inheritance, and these little places along the way are nice but not for the final achievement, which is of course nothing at all, to tell you the truth.

Here in the dunes, my alignment toward all of life and its simples came from that natural connection. It was a realigning of something in me that had been lost as I lost my way. I was compass-less and alone until I learned how to become connected with the forces of life.

The workshops, the events, the excursions, the dream studies, and the holy concentrations were all part of this readying force that took me into my lists of simples, my experiments with the essences. My life in the dunes became my laboratory. Hoping for a greater understanding, I really did try to put it all into form. Pattern helped but only went so far, because it was visual and therefore (at the time) seemed dependent on sight to exist. I was wrong, of course. Pattern does not at all depend on sight to exist, nor does sound depend on hearing.

The inner being who has all the inner senses awakened can find a way to understand life and to retain it. I discovered that I was, in fact, giving all my essences, my carefully prepared and decocted substances over into an insubstantial state to be received by this inner being.

This is important. What I mean to say is that the substance was only the signifier of something the inner being could enjoy through the inner sensorium. I was offering to this inner being all that I saw, touched, smelled, tasted and heard. And in return, this inner being began to offer me an understanding of the origin of all this, and its operation on the subtle planes.

These were some of the thoughts that I had swirling about me as I wrote my lists, carefully accounting for the date, time, place, and influence. I found all my pages about the dews, early days collecting, some images, some drawings of locations, and lists that included the season, the weather the night before and the conditions at dawn. I also found lists of my feelings in relation to all this but didn't have a clear idea of how this would be of use to me or to others.

The whole idea behind a *Book of Secrets* is to retain experiences somehow so they can be of use to others. I thought about the work of a secretary, and realized that this was what I was, simply a secretary, or perhaps even an accountant, not counting money but valuables. How many days of light dew were followed by days of heavy dew in relation to the moon, the season and the climate? How much time did it take to gather the same amount of dew on light days as on heavy days, and was that amount a realistic expectation? How was the dew to be used, or kept?

I found notes and visionary explanations from various experiments from long ago. In the old days, when small groups of people were in one location or roamed one area only, climate and conditions were varied but familiar. The plants carried the influences the people needed for sustenance, healing, celebration, and ritual. And so did the animals. The people were also made of the same stuff as these places and everything was part of everything else.

The complexity is boundless now, as everything is far more myriad and variable. The charts need computers to sort, keep and assess them.

We need the simples of our own land to help us reset our being. With their help, we resonate more perfectly with the songs of the stars. When we become able to receive the tones, they then pierce through the pollution surrounding our planet to give us vibrations that have been part of our lives since time began.

INSIDE THE CAVE

Working daily on the essences, noting conclusions for the Book of Secrets, I found my dreams brought in otherworldly experiences that sometimes were more real than daily life could ever be.

In dream, I travel to join others in a group cave experiment. We begin with basic integration and move into the cave together. To be inside the earth without any of the vibrations from the world above gives us a freedom. It is a resonance. Our own energies in feedback return on us, play back to us as if we are speaking, even when we aren't. Old shards of funerary vessels from the people before and the animal skull on the high ledge seem to observe us as we find our way into the main chamber. We know the ancients rubbed bear fat mixed with herbs upon their chests, foreheads, temples, and at the back of the knee.

Our shaman set out different ritual pots that had been in use for generations. Each of us is to place on another's forehead one of the 5 marks known from long before our great grandparents were born. There was a flute, but no drums. Song and a stringed instrument. Our oil lamps were lit with scented oil. Amber placed with flowers, the cigar left burning by the candle, the back of the cave looking like a spine.

The grinding of the ochre was like the sound of the universe heard in space, a roar of the vortex of all.

Inside the cave we feel we have connected with the root of something so significant we didn't dare name it. In emotional tones, our shaman leader cries to his helping spirits, telling the woes of his people and of all humanity. Calling that we need help and cannot be left alone. It is more than prayer, it is the cry of all humankind. Then we sing, first one, then the others join us.

Some voices sound like the cries of animals, but there are no animals present. Maybe this is the way the sound echoes back to us, given the shape of the cave.

There are other feelings there, too. Two people need to leave, two others want to go further in, to explore other parts of the cave. Someone sits and meditates. Another is in communication with a friendly spirit, who wants him to stay a little longer than anyone had planned. The shaman focuses us back to our task. We are to join together in a microcosm of humanity, to acknowledge and invoke the spirits of the animals and plants no longer alive on the earth, and whose species have forever gone from our biological being.

It is a memorial invocation of the essences of the beings of old. Much as the old saga-singing poets knew of the giants and the times in which they had lived long before. We are remembering animals and weather we had known in our younger days, or that our grandparents had told us about but that we have only seen pictures of, if that.

Sacred smoke was on all this, smudging the pathways for all. That is what we did. While we still could. For we were weak and not as powerful as human beings had been in the past. This is why several of us were called upon to seek and collect the essences, to find ways to preserve and to transmute.

Like yogis, we use our breath to communicate with these beings of nature, asking questions, or drawing them into us so we, too, could enjoy that essence and become more whole.

Persian miniatures show great saints as men made up of all the animals, and we, too, are that. When the animals leave us, then we are diminished. This is not speculation, but is a complete truth. As our animals leave us, we have less being in our makeup, and this is changing the nature of humanity.

When the dream ended, I felt whole, affirmed, initiated. I was collecting to become more fully human, and to be able to create a microcosm of all that is.

FIRELIGHT TALES

Faces glow around the beachfire in flickering firelight. Driftwood burning clean and sending swirling sparks up to meet the stars in the dark above.

As usual, someone starts a story round.

"A spark flies up from the fire in an upward spiral. Looking down, if it could look down, the spark sees the circle of people getting smaller and smaller, spiralling smaller and smaller until it can't see them anymore. The spark hasn't gone out, but it has become dark matter. Or maybe the opposite of fire. The spark fades and flashes out. The ash remains and falls to earth gently like a snowflake or miniature feather. The spark is still present in persistence of vision, and in its spot in the darkness, like a hole in memory. Like a hole in space. A tiny hole.

So many fires have burned here, so many sparks have gone up to the stars over the years that the space above the fire pit is filled with the ghosts of sparks. They are still dispersing further and further from the centre in widening patterns. Can you see the spirals of their uplift still there, frozen in your inner vision?

These ghosts of sparks don't appear during the day, but at night they call. Gathering at the fire pit, they wait for the new sparks to appear. In an unseen way they dance with them, circle and spiral upward with them, and catch them as they flare out. They help the sparks accept that the ash is dropping down like a grey snowflake. They show the ghost spark their dark lights. Soon the ghost spark is one of the gang. Summer nights with no wind, you can almost hear them, almost see them, almost intuit that they are here."

He raises the bottle, saying, "Ghost sparks, we salute you!" He takes another drink, and passes the bottle over to the person to his right, saying "Your turn."

"Okay. Here's one you haven't heard. Once there were people who had front bodies but no backs. These were the false front people. You'd see them at night sitting by the fire, or standing there warming themselves, or walking toward the fireside. If they turned and you could see their backs, then you knew they were humans. But if they backed away from the fire, that was the giveaway. They were visitors, here to observe.

Now some of you might think this is creepy, and you'd be right. It is really creepy. These false front people are only too happy to take our places whenever we leave the fireside. Look at the person beside you, is this the same one who was sitting there before? You always have to check. A way to check is to see if the darkness behind them seems different from the darkness behind you or your friends. Be careful if that darkness is a little too black, or maybe has a texture that seems untouchable. That's another giveaway.

But don't worry. These observers have never hurt us. They don't even harm the people who suddenly leave the fireside so the observers can have closer places to sit. I don't know who they report to or what they are looking for. They don't sleep.

After the fire's done, they pull the black that's behind them over their heads like big loose hoods, and wrap the rest around them like a comforting cape. This makes it seem like they have disappeared. And that's how they wait for fires, at night, standing there, just behind us now, looking for a place to sit, and to observe.

Some people can smell them, but I can't. They say it's like a cleaning chemical, sort of lemony and artificial. That smell probably covers something weird, some saliva smell, or other mucus. Someone told me they don't have front bodies either, it just looks that way to us.

Never look them in the eye though, because their eyes are almost all black pupil, hardly any whites at all, and when you see that you might start to feel confused or sad for no reason. We think it's best not to say anything to them at all, even when they come back night after night. They always move once they've gathered what they came to get."

A chill went round the fire, the storyteller takes a drink, saying, "False Front People, we salute you!" and passes the bottle to the right.

AN ADMIRER PREPARES

He introduced himself as Yogachittaji, then shyly asked if I wanted to study inner yoga teachings with him. I didn't know him well but was curious, intrigued by his seriousness, so I agreed. Introverted and withdrawn, he mostly kept to himself doing rigorous practices in his cabin day and night. I heard him snorting and puffing as I passed his place on my morning walks. He usually wore a simple loincloth, rain or shine, and had a shawl for the cold nights.

We began meeting regularly and soon a few others also joined us in our sessions, reading and meditating together. When the others came, he stepped back. He travelled away from the dunes a few months later, but left his meditation journal to me. On a separate page slipped inside the journal, I found his notes about preparing for our first session together.

"I'm writing this account as part of my practice in self-observation. I first met her on the night of the ritual, when we were setting the vibration against the developers. Thrilling to be involved in something like this, but since I'd been to Ella's rituals before, I knew to expect the unexpected, as she'd so often told us.

That's when the guys told me about her, just before she walked in to Moy Mell. She was interesting because...well, first, she was a woman, and there weren't many women in the dunes. She kept to herself and we never saw her with a guy. Her friend Cath was here sometimes. She seemed very self-sufficient and friendly. I made it my mission to meet and get to know her. Not at the ritual, but afterwards, when she'd already seen my face and kind of knew me as one of the group.

I shared some extra clams with her one day. That seemed to go over well. She asked me to have dinner that night. Now I'm normally vegetarian, but make an exception with clams, since they're so plentiful and easy to find here. She cooked a great clam stew. There was wine, candlelight. (Of course I'm making it more romantic than it actually was, but the lantern light did flicker through the cabin that night while we chatted and got to know each other.)

She was interested in the mystic path so I went on at great length (did I talk too much?). People around here had already heard my stories, but she hadn't so of course I opened up over wine (just a sip) (or two) and told of my travels to India and Nepal, my yoga path, my guru and how I met him, other teachers, my sri yantra concentration, my meditation routine, my breathing practices, my mantra recitations, my holy name, and so on into the night.

I think she really appreciated what I told her and I went home happy to know that I'd impressed my new friend. I'm celibate, and won't break those vows. I'd become very talkative. I had sipped a tiny bit of wine and hoped it hadn't interfered with my vibratory temple, my temple of great being. Just to be sure, I drank three full glasses of lukewarm water with some apple cider vinegar, and did vigorous alternate nostril breathing before my nightly mantra practices. I changed my routine a little, because it was a later night than usual. This was another influence that I hoped wasn't too negative. The next morning visualization went as usual, and the other practices all were as normal also, so I figured the wine hadn't harmed me. Why had I taken it into my temple? (That was how I thought of my body, as the temple of God.) Why hadn't I told her then that I was a dedicated yogi with an ironclad discipline? I've been on this path for three and a half years, and there is so much to learn and to do. I'm determined and I look forward to the kriyas; they should really encourage me. I hope to feel their effects soon.

Each morning I read from the *Holy Science*, only one sentence each day, and I concentrate on it in contemplation. In the evening I read the *Ashtavakra Gita* in the same way. At four o'clock every afternoon I alternate days, with either Patanjali's *Yoga Sutras* or the *Upanishads*. It's a pity I have to read these in translation. Of course I also do a complete routine of Hatha Yoga, to keep my body fit and strong. Life in the purity of nature here in the dunes is perfect for all this kind of practice.

She's a good sort, and although she said she does meditate, I think she's all mixed up with some strange stuff that seems to me to be a distraction from practice. If the chakras aren't open then how can anyone come to full realization? Without the kundalini awakening the understanding is incomplete. There is the necessity for the guru to truly open all the doors. I told her this in no uncertain terms. She seemed interested to learn from me all that I have learned, but I'm almost qualified to teach her more than the basics.

She's coming over at four o'clock today and we'll study either the *Upanishads* or Patanjali. It seems like a good place for us to start.

I'll clean up the cabin and refresh its energy, light some incense that I keep for very special practice and ring the small cymbals. I set out two cushions on the floor. She can use my good one, that's better, and I can use a rolled up jacket wrapped in a towel. I'll make some lemon water for us. And place the book wrapped in its silk cloth on the floor beside me. Oh we need a mat. The floor is too rough. I move everything off and set up again, after spreading my grey wool blanket on the floor at the place where we'll sit. There. Now on the blanket (much much better) I arrange the two cushions, the cymbals, the incense in the Ganesh incense holder (not lit yet of course,) the book wrapped in silk cloth. Anything else? Oh an offering, a flower or something. I go outside and take some grasses from the cove, bring them inside and place them in a jar. They just flop over. Oh no. I wrap them with some string to make a sort of bouquet, and put them into the jar again. Better, but now they flop to one side, all together. I get some small stones, and put them in, looks good, finally the grasses stand tall. It doesn't look right on the soft blanket, so I move the offering up to my table. That's better.

The table looks good. I wonder if she might want to sit there instead of on the floor. I put the cymbals and the book and incense on the table beside the jar of grasses. Yes, that is much better. I return the cushion to its normal place, at my side altar with the photos of my guru and other yoga saints, and my image of sri yantra. I unroll the towel-covered jacket and pick up and refold the grey blanket, putting it back on my bed. Okay. That is better. I move the photo of my guru to place it near the jar of grasses. Nice. Then I place my mala there. It looks like a sacred place now. Now I am ready. It is 10:30, I only have to wait until four o'clock.

I should start the lemon water. I put out two cups and my larger pitcher. Well it isn't really a pitcher, it's more of a cooking pot, with water and some lemon slices. There. Now I am really ready. Only five and a half more hours and she'll be here."

Reading this, I was taken aback to see how much he had prepared, while I had taken the whole event for granted. Also I felt oddly disturbed to see that he may have been more obsessive than I'd realized.

Yoga Study

That month we studied *The Yoga Sutras of Patanjali* every afternoon, without fail, precisely at four. I went to his cabin at first, but then he was disturbed because I was late a couple of times, so he changed our arrangement, insisting that we do it at my place. He also insisted I clean up, make a sacred space for our study. No, not a holy circle or any special arrangement. We sat at my table to do this studying. I was to wash the table and the chairs, sweep the floor, especially beneath the table, and put a small offering on the table when we began. I also made us some sweet tea which I think he appreciated. It was the least I could do, for he brought the photo of his guru and the book which he read to me out loud. I wrote as he dictated, so I'd have a copy to contemplate in my meditation that evening.

It was a stimulating time for me, with those sacred words that had been studied by yogis down through the ages ringing in my mind as I went about my daily tasks. Of course they were in English, and he apologized for that. Every time, he said, "Not having any Sanskrit we are forced to rely on translation."

I'd write down the selected phrase, then he checked it as I read it back to him, then we started our study. "I'm getting as much out of this as you are," he told me more than once.

We began to explore the significance and meaning of the words and phrases, and how they could impact our practice of meditation and our understanding of life. At first we took the words at face value, but soon our shared minds began to improvise freely, bringing in all sorts of implications, and relating to our life experiences too.

A light shone between us as we spoke. Sometimes there was only silence and we sat in perfect posture on our chairs, sensing the light within us with eyes closed.

CURLING THE TONGUE TO THE PALATE

Before long, others had got wind of the yoga sessions and had come to join us in my cabin. In our yoga study using the *Yoga Sutras*, we sat still as stones with our tongues just so. We were instructed to place the tongue curled to the hard palate, just behind the teeth. Someone told us that any slight pressure shift would make a difference in our inner circuitry, so we were faithful to this posture of the tongue.

We discussed our experiences afterwards.

"I feel it's making a connection up to the pineal gland, that pressure somehow stimulates."

"I was taught to do breathing practices to bring my concentration into the pineal gland inside the head. Not the third eye place on the forehead as if an eye were painted there. Further in the head, so it can ultimately point vertically up to the crown."

"I suppose it makes a kind of diagonal directive."

"I think of how the body is a map to reveal these inner correspondences."

"Well, we can leave all that to the acupuncturists and reflexologists."

"What interests us should be the points where the variations join, if they ever could join or at least harmonize."

"The simpler the better is my motto. Elaborating the basic geometries of each point leads to greater and greater variations. Too much complexity."

"That takes us to samyama, a way out of the labyrinth."

"Yes, what intrigued me about the yoga sutras was the description of samyama on various objects of concentration."

"Right! Intuitive linking with the source of the object until it speaks its name."

"Well, Patanjali didn't say that, instead he said that the object of samyama is revealed to the one who practices it."

"How does that work exactly?"

"Holding in thought the essence meaning and presence of any object we concentrate on can reveal its true and inner nature."

"So from there someone can go further and begin to work with the simples, since the essences can combine that way."

"That's how a poet works with words. Not just letters, but the magic of the words themselves."

"Then to add rhythm and sound traditionally used by the poet's people."

"I wouldn't say 'add'. It just comes that way."

"We could do experiments with samyama of objects, their poetry, find their essence."

"And messages."

Falling silent we let the conversation fade naturally away.

Here in the dunes, linked to the moon, to the earth, and to the seasons, we observed the natural changes in and around us in the moments, the days, the nights. All this was heightened during our yoga study.

At another session, my yogi friend had a book outlining the swarodaya with all the charts meticulously laid out, revealing the breath's progress and reversals in emphasizing one nostril over the other throughout the day. We pored over the notes to discern the meaning of this (to us) obscure yogic science in relation to our own elementary practices. We looked at the basics of the alternate nostril breathing, the rising of inbreath in the sun or the moon, the flow of outbreath in the sun or the moon, the harmony of these in relation to the time of day, the place in nature, the seasons. Very like the charts we used at the Essence Atelier.

Naturally this led our discussion to the sources of Indian music, the sounds of nature and of the animals, and then the human families of the ragas, their relationships between the notes, and the time of performance of the improvisations during which entire vibrational worlds were created, sustained and destroyed to be reborn again.

How they inspired us to wish for such an art, such a time as this, such a refinement that we had not known.

To some of us it was more than a pity, it was a source of righteous critical anger that this fragile sensitivity was no longer fostered or taught.

No longer respected, this refinement was disappearing from our world like the endangered species that were leaving their embodiment on the planet forever. Memory, only, survived.

"And now where's the memory of those improvised worlds?"

"They can't ever be found again. They were created through universal participation in the open art of an individual singer or player."

"Notation couldn't keep it. The act of notation already killed its spontaneous spark."

"What about recording?"

"I doubt the recording could hold its subtle vibrations."

"The memories and stories of some who had been present were the only way these experiences could be in some way conveyed, but even so that was not always accurate. "

"I think I know what you mean. If someone had been present during a master concert, for example, and if that person were ready to receive... by ready I mean, without pre-conceptions or any conceptions whatever. Then the imprint of that musical experience would be upon that person, transforming their DNA, and the impression would pass down through the generations to come."

"So the listening becomes a recording device?"

"Exactly. That impression also could be transferred to anyone else ready to receive it. Not in a musical form, unless you were a musician, but in the form of human resonance."

"Wow. Are you saying that contact with someone who had been present at a pure event could activate another human being?"

"Yes. Via mirror."

"Transmission happens in many different ways, though. Poetics, drama or the arts create a sort of replica. This can be filled by an individual or group at any time, so it becomes living."

"A DNA memory transmission."

"With living persons as playback, right?"

"Not always. Even reconstruction from notes can open subtle vibrations that inspire."

"Of course ritual triggers this, too. It can transpose time and place."

"We transcend the limits of the everyday, flying above time and the denseness of the earth."

"This isn't the only way though. Any awakened intuition can leap over time and make all connections, even without a living human representative."

Our discussion went on into the night. In us were all the various viewpoints and questions rising and falling like waves in the sea, crashing to the shore, moving us all into ecstasy, making us wonder, making us angry. Sometimes slapping us down hard until we learned not to turn our backs on the oncoming waves. Instead we faced them fully, ready to receive the gift that comes from this natural power.

STUDENT OF ALCHEMY

Later that year, on a midsummer morning at another cabin, Cath stepped over the threshold of her cabin door. She had come again to the dunes, ready to stay longer than last time. Greeting the day, she was a student of alchemy as she purposefully stepped out to collect the dew. It was a little later than usual. Kept up late by the loud partying the night before, she was not as alert to the quivering droplets held on the leaves of the dear plants near the ground. Shaking her head to bring up a little clarity, she carefully crouched, and poured the holy droplet from the leaf into her tiny glass collecting tube.

"What's the point of all this?" she wondered. But still she continued. Despite the flash in her mind's eye: all the glass tubes with their stoppers in place, with their labels tidy and affixed to the glass, perfectly lined up in their stands. The back of a hand, connected to a powerful arm, moved deliberately across the shelf to smash each of the carefully arranged and articulated groupings. Gone. All gone. The tinkling of glass. But why would she think this? There was nothing to indicate any such intrusion.

"I'll forget it, and carry on as usual."

Something darker had come from the emanations at Moy Mell last night. There were more fights than usual, and so she went over there to survey the damage. Leaving her cabin, she thought for the first time ever in her stay there that she should lock the door, or at least put away some of her valuables. Out of sight.

In this way the portents came into her mind, but not with any pressure or significance. She didn't change but carried on. Of course she was aware that the dew collected after such an event could have concentrations of the vibrations of the night before, but here the natural environment was so strong and purifying; she knew that there would be few lasting energies held there. It seemed that perhaps she should let today's batch go, but then remembered that this dew would be useful for another experiment, working with gemstones.

A few tiny gemstones were all she had, but knowing that they were able to focus energies in helpful ways, she could use them in these early stages. It was said that the size of the stone didn't matter, it was the purity that counted.

Cath had come back that summer to try to focus specifically on gem essences, and was working with them in combination. Her savings had been spent in gathering the seven major stones she wanted to work with, and her notebook was filled with studies, information others had compiled. Luckily there was a small cabin she could use. When the sculptor finally went to school, Gord had stayed on for a time, and when he left to travel through Europe with his girlfriend, Cath moved in for the summer. It was comfortable, and just enough. A few coves down from my place, which was good. She didn't want us to spend all our time together. It seemed that our essence studies had branched away from each other.

We supported one another like sisters, and just like sisters, we didn't always get along. Freedom from the perceived impositions of each other's expectations was won by argument or by withdrawal. "We're so close that we can't seem to find another way to be free," she once told Gord, when he asked her why we were so close yet so quick to argue.

Still, I was the first one she told that morning, when she returned from Moy Mell, excited, eyes wide.

As the dew resonated the intensity of the Moy Mell event way over on the other coves, Cath thought it was a perfect time to try using dew with stones and comparing their vibrations. Of course testing the vibrations was fraught with difficulty. There were no finely calibrated instruments yet invented to scan or test, so it was up to the human being to sense these. Or a cat, a bird, a sensitive dog, some animal trained to sniff out anomalies. She was to be the test subject, even though she was more than aware that there were others of far finer calibre than she could ever be. Her yoga practice was slight, and her sensitivity was not always constant, but shifted with the moon.

She took heart in knowing that the experiments done by others in this regard were equally unregulated, and equally without a stable basis. All anecdotal, all relative, occurring as they did in the changeable motion-filled universe, with all the effects and transitions that a living organism naturally embodied. So, how can such work ever be done? Notation yields averages, and perhaps these are a clue. These thoughts she was mulling over were silenced as she came over the dune toward Moy Mell. Indeed it was a bit messier than usual outside, with a few pots strewn about, along with a pair of shoes, and some clothes on the threshold. The door was open.

She tiptoed inside, calling as she stepped: "Hello, anyone here?"

Inside was dim, and a bit wild. Obviously the party had gone on too late for revellers to even consider washing up in the lamplight. Plates, cups, crusted food, cigarette butts and empty bottles attested to the night's revelry, along with some half-open books, sweaters and jackets draped on the chair backs, and some broken glass near the door, partly swept up but then left under the broomstraws, with the broom leaning against the door jamb.

"Hellooo..."

Still no answer. Then Ella emerged from behind the partition, patting her hair and pulling at her shirt.

"Well it was quite a night!" she exclaimed, "As you can plainly see, the poets were wild afoot throughout the night. Without a stop, they sang and recited almost till dawn. And fought of course. No one was badly injured. Have you seen Tickle?"

Tickle was her long grey cat, truly one of the longest and greyest cats Cath had ever seen, with cool amber eyes and a distant air.

"Oh, no wonder she's in hiding. I'd have left too if I'd had the wit."

After Cath explained that she'd come to check on what had happened last night, having heard the loud crashes, and all the yelling, Ella appraised her with piercing eyes. Just stared, as if it were none of her business. And rightly so, it wasn't, officially speaking.

Cath stammered, "I mean I just wanted to know if you were all right or needed anything."

Close-lipped, Ella clipped out a very sharp "fine," turned her back, then composed herself and smiled, "I'd dearly love a cup of coffee, dear, would you join me?"

Cath felt she couldn't refuse, not then, for Ella was like the queen of the place and Cath had only just got there. As the water boiled, Cath stacked plates, cleared the long table, and made a place for them to sit.

"No no dear, out here, in the light of the day. Let it purify us."

They took their coffee round the side of the cabin, where she had set up a small patio arrangement with some chairs and a rough table, over near the wood chopping area. It was cool here later in the day, when the sun hit the other side of the cabin more harshly, and the shade was very welcome on those hot days.

"Now let me tell you about the real Moy Mell, and how it came to be...." She began, and Cath was fascinated by her lyric voice telling tales of such wonderful Gaelic folklore that Cath could hardly believe she was still alive here and now. Listening, she was literally transported to this other land, a green place of such wonderful magic, deep battles of good and evil, and heroes who gained the sword or the diadem or the golden orb, or the special stone. "… and so that is how all those who have told the tales have been rewarded, for they are now forever living in Moy Mell."

TIME FOR PRAYER

Strange dreams filled my nights. I needed to restore my inner resources. Needing some serious prayer or invocation, I entered back into my solitude. In daytime trance, I travelled.

This time the territory was unfamiliar. Darkness, like a void, surrounded each object of my examination and contemplation. It wasn't ominous, yet, but it was evocative of nothing. Dread, darkness and pain seemed hidden there.

As my inner eyes scanned the room like a flashlight in an attic, I was conscious of being observed at the same time as I was being the observer. Unsettled, I had the distinct impression that the objects or events I was highlighting were, in fact, surveying me, through my regard of them. I felt I was creating them as my creatures at the moment I saw them, and they were bonding to me through this mutual regard. I didn't want to be influenced by their grip. I was afraid. Even though I had no voice in this realm, I cried out for help.

Immediately my light showed a small stack of books in the spotlight. Looking closer, I saw they were strange esoteric books about the soul and its journey. All told about the life after death and some conveyed weird mediumistic messages. Written in the mid-late 1800s, their illustrated covers and frontispieces depicted dramas of the soul's experience and unfolding in the return journey.

"But wait," I thought, "I'm not dead yet. This isn't the afterlife for me. I'm an observer here. How did I end up here?"

Looking around, I seemed to recognize this place: a dark crematorium.

The books came from the small apartment downstairs, where the crematorium manager had lived until the business closed and the place went up for sale to developers. Before the building had been a crematorium, it had been a large stately family home that commanded a stunning view of a river valley.

Those sent to the crematorium no longer saw that valley view. Their eyes were closed, bodies immolated. They were either travelling, or had become fixed in the pages of mediumistic 19th century books on the migration of the soul, books that called forth ectoplasm and the knocks in the night that the spirit world brings to earth. An image reminiscent of Blake, where the soul lies above the grave. One cover in gold proclaimed, *Death Does Not Exist.* And another, *I Died and Returned*. My personal favourite, *Is the Answer to be Found Across the River?* boasted an engraving of drowning souls waving for help in a silver sea of remorse.

I wasn't able to see how the appearance of this former crematorium or these books were the answer to my own cry for help. Then a picture came to my mind from the frontispiece of *Never Say Never* by Imogen LaGrande. A sweet soul in a nightie shroud knelt at the base of an alabaster statue of an angel whose wings were widespread, hand outstretched in mercy. An angel. Okay, I felt a little comforted, and looked around for more clues. I remembered that behind the heavy curtains were windows that overlooked the river valley. I opened them, and to my surprise it was not midnight at all, but broad daylight.

The light of the sun shone into all the room's nooks and crannies, and the shades disappeared from the shadows.

"Oh thank God." I said to myself. In great relief I contemplated what happened, where I was and how I'd got there.

My later notes on this had only these two summary points: I had been looking for the essential meaning behind things. The place was no longer being used as a crematorium.

THE VISITORS

It was after that visit to the crematorium that I began to meet the visitors. I first saw the lonely child, with dark circles around the eyes, weedy torn garments. Pleading. Dull-minded.

"Who are you?" I asked. A flood of contradictory answers came, in many voices, many languages. Pleading, crying. Voices from down through the ages when survival was the imperative.

Above my head this little one appeared and immediately hid herself away. Shooting out a hand to grab, shooting out a foot to trip. Laughing at the pain of others. "You see, you see. You have no idea what it's like. You see, you see. There is only my open angry need. Don't you dare touch me with your soft cushy hugs. There's a dangerous maze and I'm hiding there. You can't find me. If you do I might kill you. The closer you get the worse it will be for you. Keep away and you won't get hurt. Come closer and I guarantee you'll wish you hadn't."

I come closer and there's the baby. A starving dirty crying baby. Closer still and here's the little soul who came in hope to be embodied and to give the gift. Who did this and why?

I took the dirty baby in my arms. She had cried herself hoarse, sounding like a little animal. With a bowl of warm water and a gentle cloth, I wiped her clean all over. Removed the stiff encrusted clothes and threw them in the fire. Wrapped her tight in a soft towel, rocked and held her, then found a way to feed her. By the heat of the fire, and the warmth of the love and the power of the food, her cries became less, and soon, held tight with pressure in my arms and hands, but not too much, she slept as I hummed and rocked. Looking as peaceful as any baby anywhere in the world, fed and loved. Then the towel was empty. There was no baby there at all.

Was this my stillborn baby? No, I didn't recognize her. This was something else, the beginning of a new phase of my life and purpose in the dunes.

She was my first. I burned some smudge to clear the atmosphere. People flew in from all over, especially at night. I didn't know if they were dead or alive, from the past or from the present. I heard their stories, I sent them back. To honour them I began a scroll. I just drew a little image of the person and gave each of them a name. The first was "the little abandoned one."

All that winter these souls arrived at my door and I took them in. One at a time they told me their stories, I don't know how they found me. Every one who came was in a well of woe, and I helped them disappear.

Some were passing on, I could tell, others were dreaming or praying or crying out to God. They were all captive souls harmed by the limitation of life's restriction. Then, as quickly as it had begun, it ended. The last to come in my door was a sort of angel person, a light being who said to me most clearly:

"You are one of many who do this service for God and humanity but you will never meet the others. It isn't necessary. Now someone else will take a turn. She will do it in her dreams. Now you are free and ready for the next valley in the journey. Thank you for your service."

I added her image to the end of the scroll and rolled it up, wrapped it in silk, and placed it on the shelf. I told no one, left only a brief note in the *Book of Secrets*: "Visitors may appear and you will be asked to help them find their way home."

THE GREAT SNAKE

It should be clear to you by now that I've been dreaming a lot of this account. Just like a dream's messages, it's coming to the point where it must make some psychological, metaphysical or poetic sense. But it does not. These fragments and snapshots of mind are singular and seem to have little connection to one another.

Each is as discrete and unique as a human being, or as one of the "guys" I created and sacrificed in the fire. And with as much substance. They are made from food but they are not food. They are made with love but they cannot love back. Like the lost and forgotten souls who came to me one after the other in my winter evening solitudes, each episode comes into full view, then is seen, opened up, loved and returned.

All this emerges spontaneously, actuates for a time then returns to its origin, a disappearance. Like a pageant or a parade, or a collection of rare objects from around the world, one after the other appears, is appreciated, and moves on to make room for the next.

The task or bias we maintain here is that this parade makes sense, is whole, and has meaning. Meaning not only in the fragments but as a whole body, an entity in itself. Somehow the entirety is speaking, expressing itself through the combinations of these fragments or episodes, events or objects, individuals, families, nations and cells, through the innumerable iterations of the vortex we call time.

I'd read that here is where the collecting of essences can help a seeker understand the world better. The essences as microcosms offer the possibility to move one essence toward another in order to experience the larger versions that are held by time and space. It is something impossible to do within everyday reality.

Symbols naturally have play here as representing essences. Writing, mathematics, systems of knowledge and awareness, all help us in overview to create or recognize essences of people, places and things. Essences of life's passing and histories, of the new worlds and events to come.

Reading coffee grounds makes perfect sense in this metaphysical outlook.

The world is shot through with these cohesive forces. They can be known and used as language in relation to the infinite. The essence of all, a most rare and sought-after perfume, was my goal.

I knew that through blending the essential scents I would be able to produce the scent equivalent to white light with its opposite dark matter. A scent so rare it can only be perceived beyond the physical senses. Like the nectar "tasted" by the yogis in meditative bliss, the inner scent of the essence of all is perceived within.

It is not a scent coming in on the air we breathe into the lungs. It is not a scent that comes to the sensitive nostrils in pranayama. It is a scent that is wholly from within, from the parallel inner sensorium known to the yogis and mystics down through the ages.

Here is where we have felt the workings through us over time as the great snake moves to connect our beings beyond these flashes of iteration. It is burrowing through us all and has done so forever. Described as a serpent, it is a living current that moves through and beneath our being at all times. It mysteriously progresses through all life, emerging first from within the earth and carrying with it all the animals, plants and minerals. It is the whole force of nature, coiling and uncoiling, moving inexorably through time. It has no feeling that I can recognize using human assessment. There is only a cosmic emotion that is beyond anything I could describe or know.

This great snake's scales flash from white and luminous to multicoloured fascinating patterns like the beauty of the tileworks of the Alhambra, but living, shimmering. It is massive and is larger than our eyes can see or minds can comprehend. I imagine it as small enough to be observed but this is only a metaphor to help me connect with it.

Even the idea of snake is metaphorical, or symbolic. But that doesn't mean it is inert or not living. For this snake has more life than we can ever know. It moves in a continuous ecstasy of bliss that is physically orgasmic, with sublimely pure radiance of mind, and projecting such beauty and joy there is nothing it does not embrace and love.

Is it the feathered serpent? Yes, it was once named Quetzalcoatl. Everything is it and all is in it. It is an essential being, one of the Gods. For the Gods are essential beings who hold within themselves vast realms. They exist beyond and throughout time, and live with us when we have the courage to know them. In our era, this serpent passes through us all, reuniting us, knitting us together with all life.

Something this snake understands well is Nature's communication as she sighs and ages. transforming the earth in ways we dare not see. She calls us to help her; cries and heaves. And from her calls the sleeping snake again emerges. It shows the universe on its scales. It swallows all things whole. It curls into its vortex and uncurls to rise high, only to fall again, curling and swirling its multiplicity in pattern. For all events are seen as if on luminous screens on the scales of this great one.

Its eyes beam pure light, radiated in patterns of luminescence like persistence of vision after it has moved, and it is always moving, perceptibly and imperceptibly. The ways of the great ones were known to Blake and Jung. Milton was here, along with shamans of all times.

The great voice of the snake roars through all things, and reaches a tone so high it is impossible to hear. I sense the message: *range is the key, don't be afraid, I will connect you.*

As the snake moves in arabesque throughout the meta-cosmos, from its forehead it produces round white spheres of all sizes. These are thrown off into orbits long before they open out as new worlds, new creations.

Its mouth, when it is not open to swallow the entire void, is smiling beneath the great caves of the nostrils. Eyes open blaze in beams of white and blue light, eyes closed show two lines of smiles. In the centre of the forehead, a pattern so luminous of ever-shifting beauty, emitting white orbs from time to time. Its size? I can walk up to it and into it as if it were a doorway. Or I can fuse my forehead with it. Or I can't see it at all for it is too large.

The Companion

And just then, the companion appeared one morning, walking over the dunes, easy and beautiful, relaxed yet alert. Sensitively aware of all around him, he looked me right in the eye as he approached. I wondered if he came from earth or space. I wondered if he was friend or foe. I wondered, had I imagined him, or was he real? None of that mattered, for his approach engulfed me in warmth and joy. I felt I recognized him, but I didn't know from where. A dream perhaps?

He left a muslin drawstring bag on my front doorstep. He turned from my door to face the sea. His eyes took in the entire panorama before him. He looked unencumbered by the chatter of thoughts.

I just knew that seeing him was a most significant and positive event, but I wasn't sure where to place it in my life's memories. He walked past me toward the sea, and as far as I knew, he dove in to swim. I waited by my door for him to return for his bag, but he never came back, so as night fell I took it inside. The door was never locked, so he could pick it up whenever he came back.

Having the bag there reassured me that he wasn't simply a figment of my imagination.

After a recent heavy round of intense meditation practice, I certainly didn't want to be disturbed by phenomena that could unmoor me. It was vital that I remain in balance. As they said, feet on the ground while the heart soars to the heavens, head in the clouds. No apparitions.

And I had truly been flying that week, culminating in the morning he appeared. In my mind I called him "the companion" because, well, that's what he was to me. I was so comforted to see him, even though he was a perfect stranger. Yes he was perfect and he was a stranger, but to me he was the companion.

His bag in my cabin was a comforting reminder that he would return.

"Aren't you curious about what's inside?" Cath asked me when I told her about it.

"Of course," I replied, "but it seems like a sacred trust. I can't open it, I don't dare. He left it with me but didn't give it to me like a gift."

"Well, even the police let you keep something lost and found after a certain number of weeks. When I found that money in the woods I was able to keep it for myself when no one reported it missing. He hasn't come back and he might even be missing himself for all we know."

"I'm not convinced. I have to keep it till he returns for it and I just know he'll eventually get back here."

I'd been right. In a month or so he reappeared, just as casually and with a friendly approach.

"I bet you've been wondering if I'd ever get back," he smiled. "Here I am!"

I poured him a drink of cool water from the thick ceramic pitcher, and we sat at the table. It was as if we had known each other from the beginning of time. Swept up in admiration and a sense of awe, I felt he was an older brother or cousin, someone loving and close who has known me intimately through my whole life, but who I was just now meeting for the first time. He was smooth and tanned, with brilliant flashing eyes. His clothes were simple and plain, without any elaboration. I wouldn't be able to tell you what colour they were. His hair was neither long nor short, he was clean-shaven, unlike most of the Dunite guys who seemed to let themselves go to seed as soon as possible, beginning with no longer bothering to shave. But he was so smooth I wondered if he even had needed to shave much at all. He didn't have hairy arms or legs. I hadn't seen his chest under the t-shirt but I guessed it, too, was smooth. He looked clean, pleasant, nondescript. Not handsome or compelling, only kind-eyed, quick to smile and alert to all around him.

I knew he was aware of my work and quest for essences, and he, too, knew of this task. We didn't talk about it right away, but he asked about the vials and jars lined up on the shelves. Obviously they were not food, and he also noted the old books and journals.

"Are you interested in perfumes?"

"Yes. All essences actually."

"I've done a little study in that line too," he said.

I was surprised. Was this coincidental or part of a universal intention that he would come to my door, out here in nowheresville, and be interested in the same quest? For some reason I felt calmed by the simple thought, "Now why should I be surprised? This could be the way of things. He's come for a purpose, find out what it is…."

So we talked, he stayed for dinner, then left just after sunset. As I stood at my door I saw his smooth two-dimensional silhouette walking away. I didn't know where he was going, or where home was for him. I was reeling from the intensity we'd shared. It was as if my veins were filled with smooth milk, soothing my whole being with the sweetest liquid. It was honey. The land of milk and honey. I was the land flowing with milk and honey, and this was real.

When I went back into the cabin, the encounter played back in my memory, and I wrote down as much of what had happened as I could remember.

We sat at the table for hours, as if fixed in our places by an invisible beam. I brought down my jars and vials and explained them to him. He recognized some, others were not yet familiar to him. He opened his bag and brought out smaller bags containing his belongings: a glass container wrapped in cloth, some feathers, stones, a notebook, textbook, his wallet, and a small bundle of clothes encasing a large emerald stone and a rolled map or scroll.

"The scroll is from Japan," he said. The emerald was large for a precious stone, and was uncut.

"I am an emerald man of the emerald isles," he laughed, as he brought it out, holding it carefully. He opened the wrapping cloth and spread it smoothly on the table, placing the emerald in the centre.

"Look at this," he said, and spread in a circle on the table some more of the items that had been wrapped in his bag.

A feather, another stone, smudge herbs, dried flowers, a small horn, a bit of bone, and a hand carved glyph. These he placed in a specific pattern. We looked at it in samyama.

"You see?" he said.

"Got it." I replied.

Then he moved the items to another configuration, and so forth, adding and removing, all with the emerald in the centre.

I began to hear the high-pitched ringing in my ears that always indicated transition to the higher vibrations. This time it was outside of my head, not confined to my inner senses. The cabin filled with light. We moved the items back and forth, listening to the changes in tone. It was as if they were components of a musical instrument.

We both worked in unison as our hands played the harmonies through this exquisite expression of the essences. Then the rose scented the space, the oil and honey poured from our heads down through our bodies and hands, and the table shone in brilliant light. The emerald glowed from within. Our faces reflected the green light and his eyes looked almond-shaped. He faced me then, with flat black pupils.

"Oh my god, I'm frightened," I thought.

"Don't be frightened," he said aloud, so kindly.

Reassured somehow that he had heard my thoughts, I returned to playing the instrument we had created.

What I'd seen in his eyes was not comprehensible to me. "This will come later," he told me in thought.

We'd gone into telepathic contact without words, playing the waves of the combinations and harmonies in the objects and simples. We didn't even feel joy but only played as if we were not even there. Something played. We moved our hands and selected the items to go onto the table and placed them in various ways but we were not present, only functioning.

Snakeskin, dried berries, glacier stone, jade, oil of clove, shinbone, opal. Then...

Owl wing, ochre in oil, bay leaf, apple seeds, sage smudge, meteorite, vetiver. And so forth.

I took snapshots in my mind, but in memory, not at the time. I was too involved. It was an accelerated learning of harmonies, patterns, symbols and alchemies. A theatre rich in portent and ever-shifting meaning.

One more thing: Before leaving, he embraced me fully. Not moving, we stood in what I can only describe as the sound of fire. I felt my soul surrender in waves that alternated between dissolving into nothing and rising in lion-like full power. He glanced, smiled, and turned, walking to the sea with his bag over his shoulder.

He never came back after that night, not exactly. After our contact I was often aware of him and his gift to me: the kinaesthetic ability to know the inter-relationships between the essences as if they were music and a most serious play. His thoughts seemed to beam into mine in an intertwine, an arabesque flourish on the margin of life's manuscript of events. He was observing it with me.

I never knew what he saw though, and where his travels took him I may never understand. I wish I'd had an opportunity to look at the Japanese scroll the Companion kept in his bag. Those flat black eyes remained in my memory, but they were always held in thought with his reassuring smile, and I knew that sometime I'd discover their meaning and I would not be afraid.

Secret Utopia

Somewhere, I'd read that knowledge is not acquired without adversity and challenge. For if we already know it, we don't need to learn it again. And if we don't know it, the territory, being unknown, can bring up fear or anxiety or other emotions. All those stories of the quest and conquering the guardians of darkness do little to prepare us for what we each must face as we enter the challenge.

The challenges for me occurred daily, and I didn't wish upon anyone what my life in this "secret utopia" was like. Yes the journalists seeing it from the outside called it that, or a "Bohemian Shangri-La," but those of us who lived there knew its difficulties, depth and purpose.

Some here lived hand to mouth and had really nothing at all. We were so grateful that the doctor in town was willing to help us even though we had no money to pay him with for his kind services.

Others living here had their hells externalized. The old drunks, the ones who were running away from spouses, from parents, from the law, all were in their own way fighting the demons that had sent them to this empty place. Free to live, but only if you dare. Drinking aftershave, roaring through the dunes at night, feeling surrounded by demons of the past and future. Madness and mysticism all combined. In the centre, Moy Mell, the pasture of honey. Named, it must be remembered, for the poets' afterlife.

Any of us who have known poets can attest that poetry is not what we might think of it when looking from the point of view of the Norton anthology. To enter and express this roaring stream of consciousness is not for the faint-hearted, and cannot be so easily claimed. It is a direct discipline of the highest and most ancient order, one that can confer madness, divine madness, upon the one who dares enter this roaring ever-moving onrush. In the snake that passes through all things, in the maelstrom, in the roar of the river of life cascading down the mountains, the poet can be smashed on the rocks, drowned in the rushing whitewater. There is no aesthetic observer here, calmly and with delicate hand accounting decorative thoughts for young ladies. There is only this wide roaring voice of all. Singing full, sobbing, laughing, an open mouth, an open throat, a wide conduit. Sound crafted to text to sound again. The wildness seems tamed by text but like a captive genie released from the lamp by friction, poetry pours its intensity back into the world across time and space when it is read or spoken. Especially by a poet.

The image of the happy poets raising glasses to one another in the golden warm fire-lit cabin, is seen from outside the window. Inside there is a range of human feeling more intense that wine or whiskey can subdue. They only add fuel to the fire. If the fire is love then that is the song that is sung. If the fire is anger, then swords are swiftly drawn. And the poet is killed whether by love, or anger or any of the emotions, no matter how deeply felt or beautifully expressed. In the corner the harpist plays a most ancient tune. High on a shelf and unseen, the four sacred objects glow secretly, wrapped in their bundle.

One after the other, the poets at the table that night stand to raise a glass and recite. Some say poems newly made just that very instant, others recite the words of those long passed on, down through the ages crushed in the layers of time's sediment. Then they cry, or fight, or wander lonely into the darkness of night to gaze at stars or smash their way through the brush to curse their great ancestors, or take one another to bed, or collapse and sleep head on hands at the table, just there. One has pissed himself. Another drools. Night ends again. Mice nibble leftovers on the table. Bottles are all empty, the cups drained, lie on their sides. The harpist, as she always does as soon as the fights begin, has fled back home. With sunrise on the cabin, our hostess unsteadily rises once more. Each day a little more degraded, each day beginning again nonetheless.

And so you see this place in the centre of it all, the Moy Mell cabin, has at its heart a violent maelstrom. Bohemian Shangri-La? Yes it is that. For these great ones, (and they are truly great ones) are dedicated to the service of their lady, their mother matter, the matrix of all that is, the cause of all, and in this they offer their lives in sacrifice. From this sacrifice rises a most exquisite and rare perfume. Wherever it is found, the subtle molecules of this essence become catalysts for life Herself.

She is a cruel lady who refuses all who do not give themselves fully. The most tragic are those who give most of themselves, but still are not accepted by her, and end forever begging for more. She will not love them until they love her more than themselves, and more even than their poetry. Only then does she bestow her seemingly whimsical permission, her presence, her inspiration, her glory, her devotion, her love, her embrace.

That embrace is the entrance to Moy Mell. For all these poets are already dead.

EYEBEAMS

It was mid-morning. Late morning, actually and I'd just finished all the chores. I'd hung out the washing to dry and freshened the table with spearmint picked that morning. The whole cabin was scented. I usually alternated between lemon, orange and mint, but in the last few weeks mint had been my only choice. I felt it in harmony with the plants outside, not yet flowering, with still-tender leaves. The scent opened the room and it became alive with beauty as the sun shone in.

"Hard to get into this at this time of day," Cath said.

I knew we couldn't get anything done until later, after sundown would be even better. But there wasn't much time left, so we sat together at the table with our box of index cards and began to lay them out, looking for some kind of order to create an essence index.

Sharp mint. Sunlight. Lemonade.

Earlier that morning, I'd sensed the earth, like a magnet, holding me to the surface. Like the guys made of dough, my feet are in the sand.

Most days, I, too, stand in this sand, feet gently covered in the warmth of its innumerable crystals. Looking out at the day's light, I knew my vision was far larger than the physical eyes that I was seeing with. My eyes are large because they can contain so much. I recall medieval or early renaissance illustrations of eyeballs sending out their eyebeams. With my own eyes, I send eyebeams to all I can see. I then close my eyes to draw into my being all that I have seen. It turned to inchoate darkness, then nothing at all but the wide area of chittakash, the space behind the closed eyes, the place of imagination.

Before Cath came over, I had written in my notebook:

"Is everything I am doing now actually contained there? Is it happening outside at all? I am gathering experiences, condensing and reducing them to essence. Then I store them in chittakash until they are unpacked after my so-called death. This unpacking will expand them to a size and influence far greater and larger than what they ever were when on earth.

'Reduce to Simple to be expanded in greater purity,' the instructions had said. So this is part of the function of perception and the reason for all this interaction. Sense perception could be a sort of recording or storage device that enables God to purify the world. Just as the sun purifies all that its rays fall upon, so my eyes purify all that they see by the mechanisms of insight and memory that condense perception."

So much of the world is unseen, it is only what faces us that we can see. The back is all dark and invisible. The face of the darkness shows in a likeness that we can comprehend and understand, but the unfathomable uncreated is by far the greater half. This is where I travel."

In the context of that morning reverie, this pragmatic work seemed flat and useless. We had to deliver the list by the end of the week and had only just begun to make sense of it all. Cath wanted to be sure we got our list to the Signification Group before month's end, so they would consider verifying within this year. We didn't want to wait another year, knowing how everything changes so easily, and an entire year would certainly bring more change. We were up against the wall.

To be in the annals would be so affirming and encouraging for the work. I know her push to get this done by the deadline was also a way to subvert an old tendency I had: I didn't actually trust myself enough to complete without this external push. I could become distracted and leave this whole endeavour for another project. Not intentionally. But let's face it, the beginning is always the most exciting. It's later on, in the slog of it all, that we look for a way out. That's when we cross the fence to see the same landscape we just left behind, imagining it's different because it seems new.

So I made us coffee, and we spread the cards out on the table. She made the grid, and I began sorting the cards into their type: location, time, season, result. After lunch we outlined our next step: discovering top notes, base notes, heart notes for each when they were combined with other essences.

THE EVENT THEATRE

The events are all precariously metered out on a very light thread, hanging one at a time in the sequence set out for them. Each a pearl or jewel in its own right, each an entire world when examined in samyama. The mechanism's wheels and gears move to release another droplet on the string.

It hangs above the empty stage. It drops one event-world at a time into the light, and reveals itself to the unseen audience in this darkened theatre. The audience gives out a small gasp that can be heard from the wings each time the mechanism begins to move. They know and anticipate another jewel on the string. The lights adjust slightly to include this new addition shining a brighter light on the top new event, while the earlier beads are fading into the darkness, down to where the string eventually coils gently on the stage floor in a spiral formation. The top beads on the string are brilliantly lit up, the bottom spiral is also lit, and between these two the string is visible but shading toward darkness.

To help the audience see the spiral on the stage, mirrors are cleverly placed to show a vertical reflection of the entire spiral pattern, for it can't be seen unless from the point of view of the top of the string.

The mechanism groans, another world is born, another world is added to the spiral. The audience gasps once when the mechanical wheels begin to turn and that sound is heard again, when the new world-bead shows itself, dropping into view. Then another gasp when the old world bead touches the stage floor, adding one more world to the pattern.

There is no intermission, but members of the audience are free to come and go. We can hear the doors at the back of house opening and closing. A narrow vertical shaft of light is visible as the doors open and close. Backstage, the stagehands work tirelessly through their shifts until relieved by the next workers. It is a boring life for them. The work is set and never varies. After a year or so most of them move on to other work in other theatres. But one or two remain to work there for their entire lives.

They don't remember when the play began, no one does. Tourists come because it has had such a very long run, but it is always a disappointment. They sit waiting for something to happen. Gasping along with the others at the appropriate moments, they soon become restless to leave the theatre. Being tourists, they have to make the most of their time and really can't afford to miss some of the other attractions.

There are some who come to the theatre every day, and have documented all their thoughts and impressions. Some expect at any moment there will be a disruption, the spiral destroyed or messed up, or simply overflowing, or the mechanism breaking, or a world somehow stopping its appearance to make way for actors, perhaps, or a solid story. They fantasize alternate plays while watching this one, or when they sleep they dream of this slow release.

Old timers don't pay such focused concentrated attention on the beads or their sequence. Content to simply be there in the audience, some bring sandwiches, snacks, coffee in a thermos. Others can be heard knitting; the clacking of needles comes from the upper left corner. There are specific areas the regulars congregate in. The front row: all highly concentrated on the work and the stage events, such as they are. Mid to back of the house: regulars and old timers with food and drink, some with papers. Left back: knitters. Right back: note-takers, some with flashlights. Many note-takers are also in the front if there are any seats available. And so it goes. There are dogs allowed, but no one brings children, they'd be bored in two minutes. Meditators, who sit left and right in front, close their eyes for most of the show.

Tourists buy postcards and brochures of the play to send back home, proving they were there. Well I just have to laugh at all of it. It is a serious production, mind you, and a real part of theatre history.

Someone said that in the past, a village or somewhere, people gathered in the square and someone stood on a high platform there. Actually the same platform was also used for public hangings and for important announcements. Anyway, someone stood high and dropped beads on a string to indicate worlds, and through three days and three nights the beads were let down one at a time, as townspeople observed and chanted an old song no one knew the provenance of, sung to a melody much older than the words. The beads formed a spiral below and at the end of the three days, a festival began, while the spiral stayed on the ground marking the sacred centre of the celebrations.

The play was even older than that; for in the times of the temples, and before then, designated shamans would stand with arms held high as a snake of beads was passed from hand to hand. Standing shoulder to shoulder, assistants threaded this bead snake through their uplifted hands until it reached the highest one. He let the end drop, and then all following world-beads dropped one at a time, in measured pacing, down to the cave floor, or in later times, the temple floor. The helpers who were novices came from behind to guide the beads with their hands to create a perfect spiral.

In some of the later temples, mosaic tile was placed in the spiral pattern, and on the days of celebration, the beads were placed exactly on that pattern.

A booklet in the theatre lobby, available for sale to tourists, includes an illustrated account of this history. Some of the old-timers dismiss it as speculation, others were involved in researching and gathering the articles. Standing in the lobby, I idly flip through the pages after nipping out to the washroom. I hear the mechanism groaning, the crowd gasping. Careful not to let in the daylight as I open the closed theatre doors, I rush back to my seat.

World Beads

The episodes falling like world beads on the string, what did they mean and why did I see them? What happened later to the worlds coiled into a spiral, sleeping there?

Some dark obsidian beads carved in maori formations

One or two plastic bubbles, they can't last long

Some with delicate elvish script

Some with polite tasteful markings

All colours

I saw them all, I went into each in samyama. And a picture of life formed in my mind's eye. Then, suddenly exhausted, doubting, I asked, "Why is this here? What am I doing here? Who am I? What is my role as observer of this? Why should I do any of this?" And so forth. Answers formed in my mind as visions.

The line of beads shone in light, they slowly dropped downward to their root spiral. Behind them, beyond them, above them, beside them, all was in total darkness so thick, palpable, I didn't dare reach in and touch it.

I recalled my ancestors, all my mother's mother's mothers and saw them standing at my left, in a long line that stretched if not to infinity then at least to the beginning of it all. And at my right was a line of my father's father's fathers going as far back as I could envision or imagine.

Behind me, the darkness waved with all the good that ever was or ever had been, stretching infinitely at my back, and at the backs of all the mothers and all the fathers. Before me, between me and the line of world beads, I saw my enemies and all the enemies of everything that is good. And so, I bent my knees and bowed my head. Placing my hands on the gentle ground beneath me, I prostrated fully, looking not at the enemies but at the line of beads. In that moment, all enemies were crushed by the power of good for all generations. A transmutation of all darkness into light, with human power pouring down in prayer and devotional prostration. I stood up, and all stood with me. We bowed down again, all together.

The beads shone in the light and glowed as they received this obeisance. Surely this would sustain and renew each of these worlds. As each bead came down, I bowed in full prostration. Innumerable beings bowed with us, and it was as if the worlds were sustained. There was no one else there but us, and with whole heart we bowed. I prayed that each world would be given the chance to fully evolve and express, that all beings in each world would live in freedom and come naturally to realization.

Then it dawned on me: this could only happen because the absorptive darkness was able to contain this process, and protect it from dissipation. It held us like a dark mother. And I offered prostrations to the space between the worlds in honour of her.

As the dark mother held me, I knew she was the medium in which all light shone. As we bowed, we were swimming through her dark ocean. The lines of prostration left light waves of persistence of vision, all down along the way. Without looking behind me, I could see it even as I participated in it. It undulated and moved like a living river of light, or an illuminated snake. Our devotional prostrations were its life and motive power.

The snake of life worshipped the snake of the innumerable world-beads.

So I travelled by thought and meditation in this mythic cosmos, this infinite land of chittakash. When I notated this experience for future reference, I was astonished to discover that the world-beads existed on a scale I didn't entirely understand and couldn't actually imagine.

SUCCESSFUL BUSINESS?

Okay, so it isn't exactly easy to pull all of this together for you to understand exactly what happened, how it happened and then how we were changed by it all. Most of what we did happened inside our own minds, but then the effects began to show outside of our internal experiences, and that is where we are now.

The gem essences became a great success. Cath produced a homeopathic line of tinctures too, for other subtle healing. From her investment in the initial gems, she produced many batches. She used her own experiments and her experience using the essences as the basis of the instructions that buyers were to follow.

Then Cath ventured to Los Angeles and connected with one of the buyers for a specialty shop dedicated to the exclusive and rare. With Tibetan bones, masks from Borneo, aboriginal Australian digeridoos, African carvings, and the like, along with skulls of tiny animals, rare books, and esoteric paintings, her gem essences fit right in. Marketed at a "luxury price" soon the "Gem Essences by Claudine" gained a reputation as a fountain of youth. She also made a line of Gem creams, using gem essence as one of the ingredients. To tell you the truth, I don't believe many of her customers were able to tell the difference between the vibration of the sapphire and a stick of wood. It was kind of wonderful that Cath was able to pull it off at all. And for those who accused her of being a fraud, she had her own document of experience with the essences to prove that indeed they did hold such properties, only perhaps unavailable to those who were not yet ready to perceive them.

A well-regarded Los Angeles swami had been given one by a devotee who was also his major patron. She had been using the droplets as a face vitalizer and thought the swami might appreciate the fine vibrations.

"Ah gem essences," he said, "I recognize these from my homeland. Yes, this looks accurate." After he meditated with it, he found it to be sound, and soon gave the essences his stamp of approval.

Now the many devotees of this particular swami were thrilled to find something to buy that they could also use to enhance their spirituality. The store was inundated with orders, and Cath was happy to supply them. To think that the little vials that she placed in the sun on her windowsill in the dunes would now be here, nurturing and invigorating the wealthy with fine vibrations and subtle influence; well it was something for all the Dunites to talk about. When Cath was interviewed by the LA press, she kept the dunes a secret, and didn't tell anything about where she manufactured these small batches of artisanal drops, only available from one exclusive store in Los Angeles. Soon there were orders from England and from Spain.

Cath had the idea to connect the gem essences to the folklore stories that Ella told. It was a bit of a stretch, but she wanted to try. All she needed to do was find a hero or a message in one of the tales, and voila, the hero and the gem connected in a symbolic way, and it was a natural next step for the hero to link to the gem essence.

She came to me with the idea, saying, "I have a feeling your table game can help here." I was surprised. She told me that after I met the Companion, as I called him, she felt I hadn't been the same. Spending even more time to myself, I would just sit at the table for hours integrating the symbolic meanings of each tiny shift of an object. Back then it was a game that Cath had no patience for.

So Cath brought the tales over that night, and together we placed seven of her gem essences on the table. Cath thought of her small diamond as the mother of the gems, so we placed that in the centre of the circle. In front of each vial of essence we placed the gem of that essence. Then we had to come up with symbols for each of the stories, with the hero represented by a resonant object, and so forth. With metal, with herb, or with a written note with the name on it if there were no other resonating object to work with.

Once it was all set up, we interplayed the object with the essences. Soon we discovered how the story was a play that could act as a crystal merkaba or akasha for these particular forces in action as events. Cath finally got it, and realized how this table play worked. We soon saw the gem essences were only a small part of the whole. So small that she was tempted to give up on her little gem business entirely to devote her evenings to table play and the explorations it offered.

A photographer she liked came up and photographed Cath in the dunes. "Wow, what a story," he thought. I was amazed that he respected her wishes and didn't reveal the exact location to his editors. I still have the photo: Cath just naturally standing there, with the sunlight glancing her hair in natural grace. It was a high and beautiful moment.

But the big hand moved in and with one swath knocked all the vials to the ground.

It happened in a dream.

"How dare you!" the loud voice roared. "How dare you sell our secret? Have you no idea of the sacredness of this work and its ultimate goal?"

"But how else will people ever come to know it? I thought I was doing something good here, spreading the word, letting people know there's a subtler realm than the denseness of the earth. I really believed this was good." Cath replied in thought.

His hand and arm swept across the table and knocked all the gem essences to the floor. The diamond rolled away and slipped into a space between two floorboards. All the jars of dews were smashed in the same way. Cath screaming and crying, "No no no, don't. Stop. I didn't know! I'm so so so so sorry, no no no…"

She woke in tears, afraid to open her eyes and see the damage. But all was as she'd left it. Shaken by the warning dream, she rushed over to my place and told me everything. We decided that Cath should quit while she was ahead.

"From just one dream?" The shop owner asked. "Are you crazy? Business is so good for us, you can't stop now when we're just getting going with international sales."

"I'm decided," Cath said, "There is no other way."

Cath recalled an earlier dream she'd had: people who were using the gem essences were getting sick, then sicker. Their faces became mottled, and when Cath looked down at her hands, they were mottled too. There the mottling took the form of defined shapes and forms, almost like words written on the back of her hands. The words and mottling moved. It was threatening and ugly. Back then she hadn't known it was a warning dream, just thought it had something to do with her own fears or unresolved stuff.

"Oh God," she now thought, "This has to be stopped."

Everyone who knew of her work had always admired its integrity. But when she'd given it to the LA Boutique Exotique, some were a little surprised. They knew she was doing it not only for the money but also because she enjoyed the prestige.

"What's wrong with that?" she'd said back then. "It's spreading the word and making something wonderful available to others. And why should I hide away and pretend I'm not the one who did it? This is part of claiming my power."

Others disagreed, saying she was taking for herself what was actually for all. Someone had said that there would be a backlash if indeed this work proved to be more esoteric than she had first suspected.

In fact, only those who could sense the higher vibrations could benefit from these essences at all. It was as if the others were sort of tricked or duped, lying to themselves like courtiers in *The Emperor's New Clothes*.

The warning dream was helpful to her in the long run, because there were some dissatisfied customers who were setting out to sue both Cath and the shop owner. The essences had not worked for them as they had expected. The unhappy customers hadn't gone far with their plans when the gem essences were no longer available.

Cath had been protected from this legal nightmare. Or so she thought. Madame Claudine (aka Catherine) Cathcart and Boutique Exotique (owner Samuel Birk) were named in a suit soon afterwards. And there was still more. Next in line, it was her partner, Samuel, who sued her. They had a contract earlier on and she'd agreed to supply the boutique for three years, renewable automatically, or give six months notice. She found she had to use a great deal of her earnings to pay the lawyers to settle out of court. It was a huge mess and Cath had no heart for it all. Gord weighed in on what he called his aunt's foolishness, but Cath was adamant. She wouldn't continue selling the gem essences, not for anything.

She did, however, continue to create them. And in fact made even more subtle versions through blendings. These she made in very small batches of five vials each. She gave them away freely to the people she felt would appreciate the manner that they'd been made, from the heart.

Cath became a bit of a recluse, except for the occasional trip to visit Gord and do a little gem shopping with him. Once they came upon "Master Birk's Essence of Diamond" line of gem essences. "Look at this!" she exclaimed to Gord. "It looks like he's taken his own versions and done some himself."

"Oh, and its pricey too!" Gord remarked.

Just holding the vial in her hand for a minute or so convinced Cath that her old partner had left out some vital steps in his procedure.

"The substance is flat, but I bet it'll sell well, far better than mine ever did."

"Why's that?"

"Because it's missing certain significant top notes. That makes it much more in harmony with commerce and the world at large. And look, he's charging twice the price for a vial half the size! Whether it will do anyone any good is another question altogether."

"And check this out," Gord said, pointing to the label. "He actually had the audacity to say this! "Inspired by the gem essences of the legendary Madame Claudine." That's you!"

Back home, thinking about it, she didn't know whether to laugh or cry. She decided it was wiser to laugh.

MEETING GWYNETH NESTA: THE BEACON AND THE GLANCE

Just over half-way through my time in the dunes, an older friend of Ella's came to stay in one of the cabins near Moy Mell. Gwyneth Nesta had been going up and down the coast visiting the communities there, but for some reason hadn't felt right about any of them. Or so Ella said. She often elaborated and made people's ideas and motivations much larger and grander than they did themselves.

Gwyneth visited with Ella many times, but kept to herself. We knew she did a lot of meditation because some of the guys peeked

through her window and whenever they did, she was sitting crosslegged on a mat on the floor. Even at her age. Long white hair streaming down her back and shoulders.

When she first came here, in Dunite tradition I took her a welcome gift of food. As I handed her the little pie covered with my linen teatowel, she looked to me with enormous gratitude. Overwhelmed by the radiance that passed through her eyes, I stammered out words of welcome, then rushed back home.

I didn't see her much at the beginning. She never came to community dinners, but she wasn't a recluse. We noticed she had a steady stream of city visitors on the weekends. They didn't mix with any of us at all, and never stayed long. only about an hour or two before getting back into their cars and speeding off.

One night I woke at four and looked out my doorway to the vast night sky. The stars were crisply brilliant. I noticed a sort of beacon, flashing from somewhere in the dunes. It looked like it was coming from Gwyneth's cabin. Once it had my attention, it changed to a single beam, a solid vertical beam like a searchlight pointed upward direct to the night. I heard a loud crack, a boom in space and the light was gone.

Energized, I lit my lamp to write my account of meeting her for the first time. Not when Ella introduced her to us all, but later.

I recalled walking along the beach in the early morning. She stood facing the sea, her white hair unclasped, arms outstretched, singing sounds that I'd never heard before. It wasn't melodic, but more simple sounds, of birds and animals, overtones and other high sustained notes. I described it as if she were colouring the air with soundwaves from some universal breath inside her. When she sensed me watching her and turned to greet me, her eyes were blazing with a glance that penetrated to my core.

I was fixed in place for that incredible instant before she turned away and continued intoning. For a time my mind was blank as I stumbled back to my cabin. I laid down on the bed as waves and waves of an unknown pain passed through me. It was not a physical pain but something else, a sort of release, a kind of deep transformation. Something was burning away and I wasn't afraid. Not crying or calling out, I was as physically attentive as I'd been during the birth of Susannah. The fire left me as quickly as it had come. I became aware that I'd been holding myself in fetal position.

The next day I just knew it was time. She normally walked on the beach very early, just after sunrise. That morning I woke, washed and was down at the beach before 6. I tried to be casual. Turning toward me, she clasped both my hands in hers. "I am so very glad you have come," she said with tears in her eyes. "I've been waiting."

Confused, startled, I couldn't meet her gaze at first. "What do I do now?" I found myself asking her, in a voice that came from somewhere new inside me.

"Come to my cabin at 10:30 and we will begin."

That is how she became my teacher. I visited her often. Our meetings accelerated my inner growth and understanding. Sitting together, discussing metaphysics, we flew far above the little world of her cozy cabin.

"Don't write notes," she told me that first day. She said, "It is the soul speaking to soul, heart speaking to heart. No need for notes. If you wish to write later, then that is fine."

So I put away my notebook, and only afterwards would I bring it out again to notate the main part of our talk, so I could remember.

GREAT ESSENCE: LOVE, LOVER AND BELOVED

Power and beauty are found in the divinity of the human heart. Our bodies may hold secrets, but once opened they always tell us the truth. Within us the extraordinary interdimensional system of the chakras enables us to ascend the ladders to heaven, riding the snakes, forming spirals of gold, weaving baskets of light and interpetrating the patterns of nature.

Each chakra spins its universal vibrations into the uncreated void. This illuminates the life path, offering greater consciousness through the awakening of the power sources held secretly within. Once the chakras have begun to awaken, and the spirals of light have generated power to open and widen even further, they intercommunicate with one another and also communicate with the chakras of others. They shine, and bring into everyday life the divine resonance of their spheres of influence.

Creativity meets compassion in Love's domain. New worlds pour unendingly from the fountain of life in the center of the forest. All this is natural to us and is our inheritance. We may create and explore forever and yet never exhaust this divine source which is within us, always expressing itself. The gifts we receive are to be given to all of humanity in order to unfold human destiny. Time is the illusion we use as a constraint to enable manifestation, Time can be our ally. In sequence all beauty sings. In sequence, harmonies and correspondences play out the patterns revealing all beauty.

The essences ultimately return back to their sources, as do we all. Yet the refined fragrance of roses, the iridescent powder of pearl and the flash of the heart in diamond truth remain poetic touchstones. Even if, when viewed from earthly limitation, they are only in my mind, I still know they are there for me to sense, use, and know.

Doubt tells me this: *all the essences that I think I have collected through this time become illusory when seen from a broader perspective. Such collecting is meaningless. I might as well have been collecting garbage.* But then I recall, with warmth in my heart, that place of sacred offerings and the magic I saw when the stones became illuminated crystal skulls and the weather-beaten offerings became illuminated jewels.

Let us arise and go now to the Lake Isle of Innisfree, to Moy Mell, that pasture of honey of all the poets, to my imaginary-real cabin in the dunes, and to all the places known or unknown to the world where creative souls have found sustenance and solace in these dark nights.

Attar 3

FROM MERCURY TO SILVER TO GOLD

The agents for the outpouring of Love recite this phrase, "Toward the One, united with all the illuminated souls who form the embodiment of the master, the spirit of guidance."

They said, "The resolution of the work in the Book of Secrets is revealed in the vortex of star powers." If there is an essence recipe in this, I hope to find it.

The Mystery of the Notebook

In all this time, I still hadn't solved the mystery of the notebook the surveyor had left behind. It remained as opaque to me as it had the first day I found it. I puzzled over diagrams and charts that had no relation to any landscape here in the dunes. The asemic writing that referred to places was unfamiliar to me and looked vaguely like Cyrillic runes. Alongside the mapped areas of coastlines and inland lakes, there were numbers in measurements that were as arcane as the language. I gave up trying to understand it.

One night I dreamed that beneath our rude settlement was a glittering city. When I woke it was as if I had been welcomed to live in this vivid glittering silver town below. Had the surveyor been there? I remembered one of my favourite fairy tales, *The Twelve Dancing Princesses*.

There was a water bird that floated on the surface, then dived under to reappear sometime later in a completely different place in the lake. I was aware that this, too, could happen to me. I could somehow end up in another place after surfacing from such depth.

THE WOVEN WEB OF STORY

It was time to get back down to earth. I wasn't sure if I'd be returning to a familiar place or if everyday life would seem to be unrecognizable. The Sufi poets always yearned to be free, and were asking for the cup of poison. Is that what had happened to me? Had I drunk the cup of poison and died before death? "One more cup, beloved, that I may lose myself entirely," they said.

One more cup of this ecstatic wine, of this way to the gods, the Dionysian revels, the Bohemian Shangri-la, the festival of the unworthy, the poets of old. For Sufi poets, too, knew well the places like Moy Mell. Places where their poets also met together and drank the mead and wine of ecstatic union. Was this any different?

The tales they all told and shared together were world-tales, destined to become the matter of our thought and the pattern of our action for generations in centuries to come. Laying out our mythic patterns like the mosaic on the temple floor of the world-beads in a spiral, these poets sang sagas again and again to their hypnotized audiences. The repeated stories were soon embedded deep into our DNA as the songs of the people, as something that carried greater identity than even the family could.

These were tales of queens, kings, sages and warriors of old, of the great ones with their deeds and flaws, the castles and lands that changed hands from family to family, and the meaning of humanity in the midst of historic changes. This heritage lives in our song cycles, our theatre and poetic expressions. Story patterns reinforced and informed our vision and interpretation of it all. They gave us purpose and place in the world and in life.

The woven web of story covered the vortex of the abyss. Through continual repetition, this web became the filter through which we glimpsed the unknown, the unseen and unseeable.

My mind may know this but I still remember that this abyss is inherent in all things and events. It is in fact the void in which it all occurs, yet we're repeatedly told something so different.

I asked, "We are told that the abyss is counterbalanced by God, yet if all is God is this really so? And if we do exist at all, what then is our purpose? Who and what are these megabeings that are in continual interplay in the core of all that is?"

My questions were not light, and my answers came to me most indirectly, if at all. This is the root of all mystery, and my story is ultimately a mystery story. Who done it? What was the motive? How did the detective find out? What were the tell-tale clues?

Or perhaps better: a mystery play, where theatre shows that all is not as it seems.

I heard of a group of mummers who went from home to home, finally ending up at the town square, to put on a most moral and ribald spectacle, which unfortunately due to the lack of a proper theatre, ends in a tragic way. The story goes like this:

See our hero, standing on the platform in the centre of the square, carried away by his own eloquence. An actor in an expressive demonstration of the main thrust of the play. He loses his footing. No, he didn't fall from the platform to the crowd, though he almost did. If so, it would have turned out all right: they would have caught him and carried him above their heads in celebration, like a triumphant king or winning sportsman.

No, far worse. He fell, all by accident, inside the platform. The hole used during hangings had been covered with a rough loose board. As he strutted on the platform, our hero (as played by the best actor in the company of mummers) unknowingly loosened this board further. Declaiming loudly, he almost fell from the platform into the crowd below. He recovered unsteadily, turned and stepped back. A most tragic miscalculation, for as he stepped, the board loosened further and his left foot fell directly down. He was completely unbalanced for a moment. Yelling, arms flailing, he slipped down under the platform, to the hard earth below. At first everyone thought this was part of the show. The mummers all sprang into action. The crowd stepped back to give them room to save their hero.

The company climbed down, dove under. They dragged his unconscious body out into the square. It didn't seem possible that this fall should kill him, but to all appearances he had died from the fall. His head must have hit the side of the wood, and then again the ground below, snapping his neck. This town for some reason had built a fairly high hanging platform, with many steps leading up to it. It was wonderful for performances, but had proven a terrible fate for the mummer.

The mystery play ended suddenly. The actors carried his body into the horse-drawn caravan. As usual in such events, it began to rain just then. In the rain, the gay colours of the caravan mocked the accident with its paintings of laughing jesting clowns and tragic faces of long-dead kings whose character flaws had created great theatre events in the past.

"Pride goeth before a fall," someone solemnly said. They soon began creating their next show, which would be a fitting tribute to one of their own, he who had been one of the best mummers in the country. Perhaps THE best.

"His name will live forever," they cried into their ale as they improvised the lines of their new play, describing the action to one another, demonstrating movements and bits of business.

They did not write it, but memorized it all of a piece, for none of them could write, having blessedly avoided the church schools. They knew those schools took the old songs and ground them into dust.

So the making of this play had within it the echoes and resonances from all the plays that had ever been wrought, or at least all the plays that the company had seen or had made. Filled to the brim with allusion, it was like one great aphorism artfully condensed to particularly echo all the plays in which our great sacrificed actor had played the noble hero. They made this actor the Ur-hero of all, as all their heroes had been, and they gave him a more noble death than the one he had died.

Instead of showing him tripping and falling through the hole so ignobly, they workshopped several differing versions, acting them out themselves to see which had the most powerful effect. One was that someone in the audience had a vengeful heart and killed him with a poison dart. Another variation featured a complicated story of a fellow actor who was older and jealous of the young hero's obviously more powerful abilities.

In a bit of stage sleight of hand, he was shown to rub poison balm upon our hero while he touched his hand with his glove in false greeting. This proved too complicated. Another had the hero so despairing over the lost love of a most fair woman that he contrived to kill himself and so romantically died in this way. But the best one surely was the version they ultimately kept to. The play is about a play.

Here our hero is seen declaiming his lines with tremendous force. He knows that the platform was used for hangings. The audience is able to see what he cannot: there is still rope lying about on its rough wooden floor. The trapdoor to the place of descent is open, and that opening is known to our hero. He is no fool. Now fate intervenes. As he strides the platform delivering his powerful lines, he turns. Once, twice, three times, and the rope wraps about his foot and ankle. (It is almost a dance, a pirouette, a clever bit of physical business requiring an excellent actor in this role.) As he continues speaking and walking, being an actor he feigns that he doesn't know the rope is there and continues with the play. The show must go on. With an acrobatic slip, he falls into the opening.

He moves in an eloquent arabesque to fall into position: head down, with one foot fixed still to the edge of the opening. He dangles upside down. One leg is bent, one is straight. His legs make the number 4. His hair hangs down. He is not only still, he is ritually sacrificed. This is the mystery play that the mummers crafted. They repeated it many times and passed the play along to new members of the company. It glorified one of their own and made something new, something alive.

What they didn't know was that this was one of the ancient stories. They had mapped this tale upon the life of their colleague. That was how his name would live forever. But we don't know his name any more, only his story. And it isn't his story any more, but the tale of old.

The Star Illumination Experiment

I checked the sheltered spot behind the cabin where I'd put in an experiment to settle there. To my surprise, I found it was just as I'd left it. There wasn't much change in any of the substances. I'd set them out for the sun to transform and purify them. I'd tied coloured flags to four sticks, one in each corner: red, yellow, blue and green. In the centre, I placed a small spiral of tiny pebbles. Around this I'd fancifully placed the jars, in a sort of mandala circle, working from finer substances toward the centre and grosser toward the edge. There were twenty-four jars in all.

When I went back, the sticks in the four corners of the rustic garden were leaning but still standing. My jars were still upright, so I knew that even if animals had nosed about, they hadn't disturbed the process. Taking out my notebook to review my list, I looked intently at the materials to check at closer range.

I noted that they were overgrown with darking molds. They actually had changed, and some were much darkened. Others may have been contaminated before I placed them in the jars. One was fairly desiccated, another had dried out and broken apart. I described them, but I saw no reason not to bring them all inside for a thorough examination. I wiped the jars, and gave them a good cleaning before taking them in, then opened them all, ready to place the substances on the vinyl tablecloth. *Wow!* They still had their scents, some even stronger than ever. I wore gloves. I didn't have new gloves for each jar, so I washed and dried them as I switched from one jar to the other.

My index cards listed what I'd done with each of the substances before they were set out, but the notes weren't at all useful to me now. In fact, I wasn't sure where to go next with these substances now I had them. They'd been in the sun and the rain, absorbed moonlight and starlight, for a fortnight. *Now what? Why have I done this?* I went back to my notes; they only said the substances were to be purified and then observed. That was the only clue I had at this stage.

It seemed that this was one of my failed experiments, and I should cut my losses. I accepted that the experiment was a bit off the wall, but I'd wanted to see what would happen. Well, I had found out: nothing much.

Still I kept looking because I'd glimpsed something that piqued my intuition. Desiccated parts of the broken one, the one I'd cast away as useless, seemed to gleam toward me. With delicacy, I picked it up again, careful that it didn't turn to dust in my hands. I saw something that looked like a whorl, an eye, a spiral, or vortex. Placing the piece to one side I began to look for more. Sure enough, the others began to show themselves. In each one of these preserves, I saw the same eye or whorl, consistent throughout all the various substances! Each eye surprisingly the same size as the others. The more I looked, the more the eye looked back at me.

Straightening, I stood up from the table in a state of shock and walked to the open door to clear my mind. *This can't be true.* I thought. *What can it mean?*

Okay, let's look again.

The eye was still there, in each one. So I notated it. And looked again. Entranced. Not knowing what to do with them, I returned them to their open jars, placing them on the shelf, without their lids. Contemplating my notes, I wrote the following:

Star anise: ground, mixed, formed into patty, eye whorl on upper left corner. Small squash: dried, eye whorl in centre. Piece of cheese, mouse bones, and so forth - all everyday stuff, foods, found natural objects.

They had been in the garden with sticks marking directions. Sun, moon, rain, stars, clouds worked upon them. Somehow each produced an eye.

I ran to Moy Mell to see if anyone was there so I could share this discovery, and also to corroborate it. I needed to be sure I wasn't losing my perspective having been in the cabin alone for so long.

Martin came back with me and I took one jar from the shelf.

"What do you see?" I asked him, without letting on anything at all.

He examined it from all sides. "Well, mostly a blob with an eye."

"How about this one? Anything there?"

"Hmm, looks like an eye."

We went through the jars. They were all containing a substance with an eye. All of them. He saw it, too.

"What's this about?" he asked me. "They all have eyes, all the same size, but each made of its own substance."

"I know," I said, "its amazing. I'm trying to figure it out."

By this time, they were all once again out on the table, all looking up at us from inside their jars. Almost as if they were blinking.

The more I saw their eyes, the more I felt they were sentient and alive to me, like pets almost. I felt they had wishes and desires that they were communicating to me.

"I think they want to see the stars. I know it's irrational, but that's what the next step is here."

So that night I took them out to the garden. Following my early notes I placed all the open jars back in their former places, so the eyes inside could see the stars. It was an exceptionally clear new moon night, the stars shone sharp and brilliant.

As I looked at the scene, I saw in my mind's eye a beam that went from a star to an eye; one star for each eye, vertical lasers descended to each substance, connecting them to the heavens. My normal vision didn't see these lines, but I knew they were there. Something had happened, a linkup or destined contact.

This is just weird, I thought to myself, as I continued watching. In some mysterious way the eyes were drinking in energy from the laser-like star beams. Or was it the other way around?

I left them there and went directly to bed for a profoundly deep sleep.

Waking late, I ran out to the garden only to see the substances half-drowned in dew. No eyes visible. The jars held only globs and sticks and goo. *Maybe I can save the dew*, I thought. I poured off the dew from each jar, but it was mixed with the substances, impure and useless. Something was starting to smell. I dumped all the dew out in the garden. The substances were rotting rapidly now, the rank smell was stronger. I set quickly to work, dumping the substances into the compost, washing out the jars, leaving it all behind.

When Martin dropped by later that afternoon, all traces of the whole experiment were gone.

"Why on earth did you get rid of it all?" He couldn't believe it was over.

I told him about the starlight, the laser connections, and the transformation in the morning.

"I just didn't want it to get out of control. I think the process was set up just for that night of star contact, and after that, it was over. It turned. The normal putrifying process had been held back until then, and afterwards it just accellerated to meet up with where it would have been if this whole eye thing hadn't happened."

I'd spent the afternoon documenting. It seemed like a dream, and if Martin hadn't seen the eyes, I'd have thought I was having a psychotic episode or something.

But he'd seen the eyes too, unmistakably. They weren't like our human eyes, of course, just whirling swirls in mostly flat black pupils. Some had looked a little like cosmic maps, like the eyes of a blind owl I'd seen in a photo once. But they were all present, I mean really there, not just the shape of an eye, but a seeing eye. I'd had the impression that the substances in the jars lifted up just a little when the star beams hit, up to the middle of the jar in a moment of levitation. Rising to meet.

Later I drew an essence map, naming it the "Star Illumination." And I decided to take photos as part of my documentation from then on.

Arabesque

During all this time I was still quite serious about collecting and indexing essences, for I was preparing for the next level: their combinations. I'd been taught that singles were wonderful to know, but that the art lay entirely in the combinations and blends. This art may create a new essence. Each new combination reveals the way of life's creation, the ways of nature. I found many varied notes and spirits are compressed and held in only one essence combination.

I recalled reading in an old *Book of Secrets* something that I'll paraphrase here: "It is a lifelong work that cannot be achieved by any one person, at any one time. Our only hope is to open to the work of those from the past and collaborate with them, as well as those here in the present, working from the body of knowledge that is given to us as a living book for our study and inspiration."

Some of my training occurred personally, in my imagination, and was all given to me in code. All the events and metaphors were not shown to me in any way that others could understand them. In truth, I could barely understand them myself, even when I notated them.

The task before me was to take all these encoded essences and open them on earth, make explicit their implicit meaning. Unfold them.

I worried that, like the melted star-eyed substances, they could turn to smelly mush, dew-drowned and eyeless, dumped all together into compost after the beautiful task was accomplished.

But maybe, I thought, *that occurs only if there hasn't been a proper understanding.*

I asked myself, "Did that happen because I went to sleep? Is that the cause?"

The inner answer came, "There is no specific cause or one direct effect. Multiplicity abounds. One eye is as good as the other. The substances differ with variable qualities, but ultimately they are of one source and one single purpose."

I remember Ella once said, "Poetic resonances are our teaching tools. Learn the elementary lessons here. Then begin."

I was learning, discovering how to command and play with essences in a sort of arabesque of cosmic super-intelligence. Not only from abstraction to the most minimal, but from form and shape to glyph and mathematics. I engaged in a wildly messy exchange of entities, beings, forms, and ideas, all interconnecting in the ultimate interplay of our essential awareness. It was a whirlwind, highly focused and innerly directed, happening in the here and now but also in the ancient days.

What They Were

One day, in tears, I saw quite clearly what I was doing. By saving the essences I had hoped against hope that I could somehow rescue my lost child, restore her to health, so she would be born anew and live again. This time she would not die before her birth.

All the stored jars of essences were only parts of her. All the eyes were her eyes. I saw the hand that with one wide swath had smashed the jars from the shelves. This smashing of the carefully saved and catalogued dews and simples was not done by giant hand from outside, but by myself, for I was the one who had done this. And I did it now, as I realized the root of my search.

Not enlightenment, but that would have been good. Not realization, although I thought I was going there. No, it was much simpler than all that. I just wanted another chance to help my baby to live. If I had continued, who knows, perhaps I may have found a way to do just that, to infuse the substances with such essence of life to create a person. For that is the goal, isn't it? The full human being, created and uniting all the essences into one.

Weeping and shouting in anger and despair, I raged through the cabin; tearing up the pages of my notebooks, smashing all the jars off the shelves, tossing the whole lot out into the sand. Then, still in tears, sweeping the floor. My falling tears along with broken glass bits were rolling into the spaces between the floorboards. The shards like diamonds fell down, down under the house, lost, to blend with the sand. Sharp sand, now. Dangerous sand now.

And what of the *Yoga Sutras of Patanjali*? Had they too just been a stopgap measure as I desperately tried to find a meaning in my loss? Yes, just as they have served humanity down through the ages, as a hope and a method for those who need something lasting in this world of change and sadness.

Empty, spent, I looked at the world I'd created, and laughed. It was small. Pathetic really. Sure, it had protected me from the worst of my sensitivities and gave me a hope to continue living in the face of loss, but it was such a little shell.

I looked at all the people I'd found to be so fascinating here, and realized that they, too, were each running away from a part of life that was too terrible to bear. Poets with their broken hearts and impossible dreams. Artists with their inspirations birthed through torn psyches. And the drunks and con men and lovers and strange ones, all who came here to find a place that could be safe, that could nurture them, hide them, and give them sustenance. Pat who had hung himself, whose absent presence warned us of the depth that despair can drive us to.

And the Faery Queen? She, too, was far from the world; falling asleep in front of the fire night after night, while her devoted companion gently slipped the glass from her hand, and put out her cigarette, before waking her to go to bed, or just covering her for the night as she slept in the armchair. Dreaming of the great gods of yore, of the great kings and a time when there were simple forces acting one on the other, with purpose and magic.

The harp played an old air now, I heard it softly behind me. It was a tune I recognized from a time in Moy Mell, a dinner that, as usual, had gotten way out of hand. A poet cried in his drink, a communist stood and ranted on, while the invited guests from the city were shocked and appalled but fascinated all the same. That was the tune.

The union of the emptiness and nothingness united with hope and fear created this magical poetic reality. A far richer reality than those in the city could ever dream of. The shifting sands covering everything and then uncovering again. The brilliant stars beaming down. The waxing and waning of the moon. And the sea always bringing itself in waves to sacrifice at the shore, then returning only to sacrifice again and again.

This was what I had missed in my seeking for the essences, and in my collection. All the essences were here, embedded in everything, all the essences were here in my purview without any effort of cataloguing or categorization. Lists and index cards or photos made no sense here.

I understood that every one of the Guys I had made so lovingly were all my stillborn baby, each of them. And when I burned each one, I sacrificed to the fire again and again that breath of life.

Why did the one I had been nurturing within me only come this far into life and no further? Why were my breasts feeding no one? Their milk was useless, only a pressure in the days just after the birth. Which wasn't a birth, but a death. And it was the death of me. I knew that now, with complete clarity. I also knew that as I followed my dear baby to the other side, I abandoned myself on earth.

Then I'd looked at my life and decided to do something more worthwhile, something far from the mucky sorry process that brings only death: to seek what is lasting and to dedicate myself to that knowledge. So I tried to create through the essences a good and noble life. But this quest was something so personal that even the *Book of Secrets* I was writing felt too secret to share. Was that partly why I destroyed the experiments?

It was an empty time. I suppose that is freedom. Or relief. A state of being not influenced by anything or anyone, nor is it influencing anything or anyone. The great nothing. In this space of nothing, I knew I had finally accepted her death. I had let her go.

I took a place back on the wheel of life, stepping back on at a spot just ahead of the one where I had left off. I was a woman whose only child had been stillborn. A student of meditation and of essences. I joined my heart with all the other women throughout time who had lost a baby to miscarriage, still birth, or early baby death. My heart joined with the mothers who had lost children, at whatever age, even when old and the child is grown, with children or even grandchildren. I joined in heart with all my sisters who have experienced that loss and have come into the great terrible understanding: Life goes on. Precious life goes on, the wheel turns, we are on it and we are turning it. We are not dropping out and dropping off this wheel. Staying still won't stop its inexorable pull. It cannot be stopped, and if you leave your place on the wheel, it grinds as it pulls you under.

This wheel is in my heart and I am part of it again. With open eyes, I stand in my place. Younger women are to one side of me, I see children beyond them, while older women are to my other side, and I see someone even older further along. Together we are shuffling in a round dance. And we are all there: mothers, grandmothers, children, all. Now I see that I am here, in all my own stages of living, from baby to girl to teen up through the times. I carry this dance within me. All the dancers are myself.

Birth Again and Pangs

In this empty space in the dunes, I had the time, and the work, to discover who and what I could become. The doctor in town had been very wise to ensure that I could create this process for myself. He observed me at a distance, trusting in the positive effects of his natural prescriptions.

In time, I came to understand the next stark and uncomfortable truth: that the issue was not really the baby at all; it was, in fact, me. Just as I knew fully that the dread hand that swept away all my years' work was none but my own, so I also saw that the birth I was attending was, in truth, my own. It was my head crowning, my stillborn self lying lifeless on the table, quickly whisked away by the nurse to be wrapped and cleaned. She was already cold. I saw her face, and my own face turned to stone.

I remembered it all. I watched myself turning away, having no tears, turning onto my side, looking at nothing. After that my eyes were closed even though they looked open. I wore that mask for years, as if I had always been this way.

Behind the mask, I asked myself over and over again: did I somehow poison her in the womb? Was it somehow my fault that she didn't live to see the day?

Under it all, this is what I knew: I gave birth to flat black emptiness. I was a mother of death. My womb was the cave that is only used for funerary rituals, and in this place my heart froze. Everything I did or thought or tried was simply a charade of life. For at the core of things, I was carrying a black vortex in me. It was my ultimate dark secret: I carry death inside myself. I produce death.

I looked to find others with similar dark secrets within them, for with them I could, paradoxically, relax. I could be something more like myself. No one asked questions. It had seemed that I had "gotten over it" thanks to the doctor, the sun, the air, and life in the dunes. But the last step had yet to be taken, and I knew it was time to open into the abyss.

For finally I was beginning to thaw, and felt the pain that can only come from emergence from such a restricted enclosure.

I shattered that stone self forever. It was as if a hammer had come down on my head, revealing that the stone was not solid after all, but only a mask. At the instant that the hammer shattered the mask, I saw a flash of her most tender little face. I recalled what I hadn't dared to see those years ago at the time she had been born: that replica of a living baby, perfectly formed, delicately beautiful. A lifeless lovely doll. What shattered was the concrete mask that had protected my face from ever being seen in its sensitive fragile vulnerability. Instead I had worn a mirror of death.

Sitting on the threshold, I cried sweet tender tears of natural sadness and regret. *Oh Susannah.*

That face of innocence is not hers, but mine. I clearly see it is me in my own rebirth. I am ready to start again, to become whole.

The bird of darkness flies into the mist and fog and disappears.

It Isn't Me

I went to find Martin. He was at the back, chopping wood for Moy Mell. Crying, I told him all that I'd realized, and he was so kind, holding me and stroking my face to push the tears away. It felt good to be held, and understood and seen.

It was a long shot, I knew it was, but I did it anyway. Even though I knew he was a yogi and someone I'd never had any romantic interest in at all, I kind of threw myself at him. Just with a kiss, full and open and on the mouth. I suppose he was safe enough for me to give it a try.

He was kind and patient, telling me clearly, "Oh darling, I'm not the one for you."

"Oh," I fumbled. "I know....your yoga vows."

"Not exactly. I'm not just completely dedicated to yoga celibacy. I guess you didn't know, so I'll be open with you here. I'm getting the place ready for Ron to come."

"And...?"

"He's the one. My partner, you know, my lover. That sacred love you are looking for, for yourself, I know you'll find it. It will find you, like it found us."

Martin was so direct and compassionate, I didn't even feel foolish. I pushed aside the worry that I'd embarrassed myself. He was so good about it all, there was no way I could let that come between us in our close friendship.

Then he told me this, "But I've been waiting for you. Not for us to connect like that, but waiting to meet you here, in this place."

"I know exactly what you mean," I replied. "It seems I've been waiting for this time, too."

I told him about the mask, about Susannah, and all that I'd been through. We talked well into the night, hearts open and eyes bright.

It wasn't long before I felt connected to everyone there in a whole new way. Maybe, like Martin, they'd all been waiting for me to get here. There was more of me to connect with and I wasn't afraid to let down my guard and reveal myself. My door opened, people came and went. I welcomed visitors and visited them too.

SACRIFICE

So that's how I became the empress. It took time. In this lush forest, the living jungle of humanity, I saw all life glowing and growing all around me.

And I often spoke her name, Susannah, the name of the child I never knew. Surprisingly, she came into my life. Each time I spoke her name, there was more of an opening, more connection, more space. She was my *Thel*. I came to know her not in form on earth but in essence. With her essence beside me I surprised myself: I returned to my work.

I'd opened my heart, and had seen the effects of the loss of Susannah in all the ensuing patterns and problems in my life. The whole scenario had shown itself to me in time's wise increments. Once I saw the big picture, I took the next step and allowed the resonance from the realization to have its effect. I stayed on in my cabin and continued.

I was, for a time, far more free and happy. I felt I was living on another level of life than ever before. Better.

At first I'd questioned my interest in the essence work, asking myself if I was only using it to run away from life and reality. But Susannah's essence was more near me when I did that work than at any other time. When I was with friends and family, "living in the present," it didn't evoke her being beside me. But now, as I sit down to catalog the cards, or when I create combinations of the essences, or on mornings collecting the dew, she is with me. Somehow beside me, present in an invisible cloud. I don't care if she is real or imaginary, it is right for me. Life feels far more complete.

Part of me thought I was using the idea of her, but to another part of me she was truly present. I was creating her though essences and she was a goddess to me, making me a far better and more whole person.

I hadn't ever been happy about the isolation of this work, and it had always been a drawback. Now, bathed in her love, I was not only free to work, I couldn't wait to dive into it. Not because I was hiding from life. On the contrary, I was going ever more deeply into life itself. Her presence gave me courage I hadn't had, happiness I could share.

When she left me, a dark bird flew into the misty fog. At her dead birth I'd obsessed on death and my guilt, wearing a death mask fused to my being. She wasn't free to evolve or function until I was able to let her in.

I'm not even going into the deep problem that her soul is unmanifest while my soul is manifest in life as "me."

As my work led me to understand essences, she was able to have an experience of life.

Being a fine gossamer being, she wasn't able to handle the rough coarse realities of the earth. Incarnation was not an option for her. So through my love and her curiosity we came to a kind of agreement where she could use inner senses to experience refined essences. It was for her that I created the higher tones of all the essences, the finest and most unstable of them all. I did the work for her, so she could know some of the pleasures of life and sense the beauty of this world. In this way, I was her mother.

Like a delicate negotiation or an exchange of prisoners between enemies, we met on a wide empty plain. Here I would bring her only my most elegant creations. And here she could only receive those that were as far above the denseness of the earth as possible. This was the way she trained me in creation of the most fine.

I have no proof that Susannah could ever really take in any of the essences I brought to her, but I continued to try. Sensing her presence, I spoke and sang to her, happy in my work, humming away.

My earlier serious experiences carried within them the sad darkness that I hadn't yet seen or known in myself. Well, I always knew it was there but thought it was in everyone, that it was the human condition. Since the realization, I'd come to see joy as also being part of the human condition. "The bringers of joy are the children of sorrow." I understood this phrase inside out.

It is sacrifice. Did I sacrifice my child so this could happen? No. Never. It was not in my hands.

An observer from the fourth or 21st dimension or further might differ, saying that my sacrifice had been made by my own pact between my soul and hers long before, outside of earth's time. Another might say it was random chance, and there was no such thing as fate or destiny, and the molecules that clustered together to create these events could as easily have clustered in another way, sparing us but changing the direction of the flow of things.

The snake, the current, the luminous flow of life energies and events can't be decoded in linear single forms, but only through simultaneous multiplicity. Cause and effect are not reliable instruments here.

I only knew that the full activation of my heart led me to complete my quest, and my opened heart reflecting all became a resonant mirror.

The black vortex is illuminated by the light of the heart; the spiral serpent flies on its cosmic mission to discover and devour new worlds.

When I allowed the serpent to turn and devour me, I became able to see through its eyes. I can ride with it as it goes through the many worlds, now and to come. It doesn't make linear sense that I am at the same time roaring through the cosmos in the giant plumed serpent and am here in the cabin, measuring dew while singing to my incorporeal daughter. And simultaneously writing this account so future readers may follow along in the events and understand them. Am I the writer, the one residing in the cabin or part of the cosmic serpent? Yes this is a fine essence indeed, with exquisite top notes, good lasting base notes and a fascinating mid-range that flashes differently over time.

I'll sit with this essence for a while. The top notes, the highest, are most unstable. When they disappear, I'm always left with the interaction of the mid-range and the base. That's when the love is felt, love that hadn't expressed at all when the serpent, like a comet, flew through the vastness of space. That love is here at the base, infusing all with profound simplicity and grace.

CONTINUING ON

The sands of life and time shifted once more, covering what had been uncovered. I was just my ordinary self. Nothing special. Nothing at all really. There was no grand reception. The whole event and realization about Susannah hadn't made any dramatic change in my outer life. No lottery win, no sudden shower of flowers. Standing at my door, I held my arms wide open to the sun: I'm here, I'm here. And yes, I did feel wonderful. No one noticed as much as I did. I confess that at first I felt let down by that.

Oh, people were happy for me, and yes over time I did feel I could be closer to others, and certainly more loving. I was quite teary, and this lasted for about a month or so. The slightest thing would bring me to tears. They were good tears, not tears of frustration or anger. Sadness for the experience, sadness for the many others who also had that happening every day somewhere in the world. It was, after all, a part of life.

Now I was here and I knew it. There was no actual escape or fascinating new life that would take me away from all this. Into what? I brought all myself with me. So it was that I began to feel a gentle universal participation in my life's unfolding.

Then Cath came to visit the following month, and we could finally have a great conversation about it all. She was my counterpart in the world. Cath understood everything because we'd known each other for so many years, and she'd known me before it all happened. She was my friend through it all and I was so grateful to her. Even at my worst, she'd stuck by me and had not given up. I didn't know many others who would do that. Now that she'd confided in me, at last, for the first time in so many years I was able to be a closer friend to her, too.

All these events that happen on the basic level of life, our interchanges, our sorrows and joys, what Yeats called "the foul rag and bone shop of the heart," these were an essential part of the higher endeavours. Not separate from them. Yeats said this was the place where all the ladders start.

There is no true Moy Mell for any poet unless the ladder is firmly planted here in the heart. Its piercing can be painful but that pain brings the required intensity for expressing the wide weathers of the big life. We raise ourselves up that ladder to the big life, and still see our small selves down below, struggling and striving in feeling and being.

SENSORIUM AND THE ESSENCES

One night after a community dinner at Moy Mell, some city visitors were asking us about what we did in the dunes. We loved to talk, all eager to share our experiences and insights, for, strangely, we were lonely together. When it came to my turn, I first described my essence work.

"... And that was how I began working with the essences. Most of my explorations still continue. It's all part of my personal quest. It is actually an internal search for the fabled "gold" of the alchemists. I document and fit my work into that history as I create my own encyclopedia of knowledge. They call it a *Book of Secrets*. I expect I'll continue to write volumes throughout my lifetime."

"Fascinating. So, you're involved in alchemy. I'm interested in the esoteric side of things, too. Can you tell us a bit more about the essences?"

"Well, I learned that each essence has three basic attributes, or inner vibrations; these are base notes, mid-range (also called heart) notes and top. So I sense those. Then from that awareness I'm able to figure out how an essence can combine with others. Combinations are tricky, for the base of one may seem to be a mid-range in relation to another, and so forth. It's amazing."

"I heard that a high sensitivity causes all kinds of problems in everyday life. Is this true? What can you do about it?"

"Yes, that can happen. It's wiser to have a quiet undisturbed place and time of working. That's why I'm here in the dunes. Especially at first, the city, its mercantile world, opinions, empty society, and politics can make it difficult. You have to learn to reconcile these coarse influences within yourself, especially while in the state I call "essence awareness." The goal isn't simply awareness of the finer essences and other combinations. We can use essence understanding for all kinds of things."

"You've said you studied the history of this work?"

"Oh yes, always. There's a rich background to all this, and more's coming to light every day. The wise Sufis of old called it "the alchemy of happiness." I suppose my work has been for that, for happiness."

"So what would you say happiness is, then?"

"Let's just say it's not the usual definition of happiness." I paused to find the right words. "It is more about the richness of life, and finding ways to perceive a sort of inner sweetness."

I took a risk and went a little further. "You know, once the heart unlocks it remains open. And then it starts to become a sensory organ. Its emotional and meta-emotional capacity expands and brings beautiful awareness to all life."

Another jumped in, "So your heart was "unlocked" and it functions as a sensory organ? Can you explain a little more about that?"

"This is a subtle topic. I'm working on it in depth in the *Book of Secrets*. It's the whole of the work, actually." I thought for a minute, and decided to open up a little further and explain more. "There is a sensorium represented in all the essences. I mean scent, taste, touch, hearing or sight or a combination of all these. The perceptions of the feeling heart work to open a direct conduit to intuition. In turn that opens and deepens the sensorium."

"But what does that have to do with the unlocking? And how can the heart be a sensory organ? Science doesn't show that."

"This is known by the heart. Mystics have said there is a heart-conduit to intuition. In essence terms, I would say the heart adds sweeter and subtler notes. The difference is one of tone, of expansion, of love, I suppose."

They nodded and seemed to understand, so I went a step further, saying, "Then intuition kind of pulls you up to meet it. That way you can create the reality your intuition saw or glimpsed. The next process is even more amazing. You get to enter into and enjoy that creation."

Just as I was getting going on the other implications of all this, I noticed that I'd lost them. The conversational spotlight quickly moved over to the next Dunite, a would-be poet eager to read his latest work. Then we ended as usual with a "tasting," as the two loquacious manufacturers explained in detail how they made their own whiskey behind the cabin.

MYSTERY

As I catalogued essences, listing and placing them in the book, I was both elated and let down at the same time. Elated by my accomplishment, for I'd become one of the workers who had a *Book of Secrets* to leave for others. But let down because I didn't see where to go from there. The serious issue that I couldn't speak to anyone about had to do with the nature of my *Book of Secrets* in general. Was it too anecdotal? Or too hidden? It shouldn't be so occult that its mystery remained unsolved. Was I doing it right?

I considered each entry as a miniature mystery to be solved or resolved, with clues to be picked up and followed. And the entries interrelated too, so the mystery also progressed across episodes, an accumulation pointing toward a beautiful resolution. A resolve to go forward.

When a dead body is found, we always need our detective to step in and uncover who did it and why. In my case, the mystery is the death of Susanna, my stillborn baby. I knew that in any good mystery, the dead one's life secret is revealed and those who wish him/her dead are gathered in the room at the end, while the detective reveals who had motive, who had means, who actually did it. Sometimes the spirit of the deceased guides the detective to the various suspects, and to the clues.

In the case of Susanna, it may be that her people wanted her back with them. If so, then the dead were the cause of the murder, and this was a horror story.

On earth we all welcomed her, all except for her birth father of course, who took off. Was his rejection influential? Am I trying to clear my name from the accusation within myself that she died because of my dark womb or something I had done? Talking with the doctor, and looking at other cases revealed that there was no fault of mine, but I wasn't able to believe it at first. Only through the work on the essences and inner practice could I find the way to truly clear my name, and open my heart again.

I spoke with the families of other victims of this serial killer (who is called Death). It was clear no family was spared.

My mystery investigation continued on, parallel to the work on the essences, perhaps because of it or maybe in resonance to it. Each essence was one string of the mystery instrument that, when plucked, would emit a pure tone that caused all the other strings in its vicinity to vibrate in resonance, and in some cases, also to sound.

THE CRIME

I feared a monstrous crime had been committed and the person who perpetrated it had escaped. I had to investigate for myself.

Naturally, when I entered the next vestibule of sound, I was afraid.

I was looking for clues. How could it be that this world of promise had become so much a world of negative illusion? Somehow the Daddy Warbucks of the world had really taken us all for a ride, but first gave us candy to put us to sleep so we wouldn't feel the rape and later discover that our credit cards were all in their hands, along with our PIN numbers given so freely while doped to the gills with drugs and entertainment.

Anaesthetized, we were helpless victims of the barbarous vampirism: Life-force taken so they can live and remain forever young. We awaken in the husks of our formerly vibrant bodies, disoriented and yearning for a way out of hell, crying for relief but unsure of what we need relief from, or how to get it.

They built cities then, using all our life-force, and they blocked out much of the sun's vitality, and of the purity of the day and night. Awake in the night in bright artificial light we can't find a star in the sky to wish upon.

"Not exactly, but maybe metaphorically."

Open Sesame

Moy Mell was a place for subtlety of mind. It was so named and so it became.

One dinner, we talked about how naming is a secret of creation and a way to open the space. The physical form seems so solid it could not ever move, then, almost magically, with the right name, a space reveals. *Open Sesame* creates a doorway in a seeming-solid mountain, and reveals a cave of treasures within. I rushed home to write down what we'd talked about.

Every bit of solid matter can open up in the same way. What seems solid, opens to reveal another akasha, a space. All the spaces within are all interconnected and they are in fact one vast space. We can also create spaces that we can fill with our own wishes or desires, something to benefit humanity, or to gift others later in time's progress.

Magicians have hidden many such man-made caves of thought and being down through the ages to be discovered by future generations. They are awaiting our discovery now. King Solomon said there is nothing new under the sun, and this is true as we recycle over and over again the patterns of human experience.

We discovered the thought-caves. In these caves are innumerable thought-treasures. They give us integrative patterns to infuse today's life with past wisdom. This old knowledge had been hidden, lost to memory if ever it had been known at all. These caves have held secrets for millennia. We saw how writing, art, meditation, ritual, ceremony, theatre, devotion, prayer, love, dance, dream and more can open the way.

We didn't all agree, but some said that if indeed we came from space we could say that our overlords left these clues for us to discover at the right time and to survive. Science and technology have not replaced our old intuitive arts, for they are actually complementary. They offer keys to the complex of thought-caves left to humankind by great beings.

We map the caves and the experience of them in differing ways and languages. The worlds in these caves are populated by others like us yet not like us. We see the unending stream of the so-called imagination, which is a combination of intuition, inspiration and art. The spark of creativity opens the flow of creative expression, unendingly morphing into innumerable forms. Finding meaning in this stream and shaping it toward a creative purpose is the work. On this we all agreed.

For it is not enough to observe and account, to explore and convey the wonders, like the 19th century discoverers of the tombs of ancient Egypt, avidly unearthing the treasures, writing detailed examinations, lists and such, or illustrating pages in sketchbooks to share these remarkable discoveries. There was an opening up of consciousness as the tombs opened. A new way to approach the mysteries was born with this language that hadn't been made public until then. Their purpose was historical, scientific, to give the western world a view of this Eastern majesty and mystery.

But they couldn't know what the meaning was of the scarab beetle, even if they had been shown and told. For that knowledge it would be necessary to enter the space where the scarab was and, in dialogue with its depth, come into a small inkling of its meaning. For like the African peoples who had the belief that a species of ants was the cause of a particular illness, one that could only be cured by connecting with these ants, this scarab has a message and meaning in ways our worldview just can't see.

We dare not enter that primoridial understanding based on no separation. Our minds can't handle the impact of such a meteorite rushing through our atmosphere to land on earth, shifting the orbit, changing the weather, killing the dinosaurs and creating new life. We are programmed differently.

The plant medicines can unlock the mysteries. In the same way, yoga practices that stimulate the pineal gland also bring up more awareness that helps in translation of the meanings of our lives. "To know and understand life better."

This discussion was even more stimulating than I knew at the time.

That night I dreamed my hair was striped red and white. Placing my hand on my forehead, I was circling the palm over the area of the third eye, until it became warmer and warmer. I heard a voice singing in a language I recognized but couldn't understand. It seemed to tell me about interconnected akashas within, where it is all one space.

THE INTERSTITIAL SYSTEM

Although I'd written my account as faithfully as I could, I became aware of gaps and inadequacies in expression. It was clear that I was only a novice in these explorations. What right did I have to even imagine that I was writing an account worthy of merit in any way whatsoever? And so on, undermining any courage and resolve I may have had.

How dare I live in a cabin in the dunes, a place I've only been to in my depth of being, and then only for a very brief time?

That night Ella phoned me in my dream, bringing this message:

"Moy Mell will always call me, even back to where I had my final resting place in my dear home in the town, across the street from the good doctor. All my helpers were there around me, and after I left they dispersed, but now some have come back to my home, others gone into the wide world of America. We each have these. Have you found yours yet my dear friend? For you are my friend and you are helping me to bring expression. Don't be one bit afraid. There is a unicorn at my gate! Yes, just as there is a Moy Mell, and just as the dunes are still here, waiting again to transform this next century."

Then in the dream her voice changed. She spoke more rapidly. "As you may have guessed, this really IS that thing you think it is. All this works from the inner lines between beings, events, and places; that wide space is a conduit. Energy courses through and pumps to all that is, bringing brilliant light. Enter this stream. Float on it, fly with it, burn with it, dissolve in it.

"You are now involved in the interstitial system. There's a secret in all things and beings and events. It is a unique iteration every nano-instant, a fountain outpouring All, at all times, connecting to all times.

"Come with me into the interstitial conduit. It removes the barrier of time, which has been the main secret of the wise sages. Wisdom on earth expresses beyond time's limitations. The wise seer lives in such a way that time ceases to exist. This is not science fiction.

"The refined human being becomes an instrument sensitive enough to record this process. That is the inner secret of the *Book of Secrets*."

As she spoke, I saw myself standing, turning, on a vast plain, free in all directions, with blue sky wide and far above. I was a spinning top, a pinpoint in vast time's expanse.

She continued, "It is never late, don't you see? It is always now here. You are connected to all and at the same time alone."

Standing spinning here in the vast space, all alone, I heard her voice ring through clearly.

"Now don't think too much. Let the essences lead you to understanding things in their simplest, emptiest, and most iconic. See them as symbolic, seminal, essential marks or pinpoints in space.

"We meet others here in this way, and the connections so made last longer than lifetimes."

I woke, but the messages in thought continued.

"Waves of bliss pour through the body and the mind is completely aware as a perceptive organ, not at all as a barrier to experience. This is the love. This is it."

SUBTLE SHIFT

After Ella's call in my dream, the shift was subtle but significant. My reporting on all the experiments and activities took on a greater presence and I was more confident and assured.

The events and experiments became less personal. They were more open and accessible as activities. A voice had come forward. My work on the *Book of Secrets* expanded, and the study of the essences opened further. I'd come into the second phase of the work, something I'd read of but had never known myself, nor had I imagined it coming to me.

This was one of the esoteric sides of creating a *Book of Secrets*. As the guidebook said, the act of producing such a book is also an initiation.

Sincere seekers throughout the ages have discovered that there is a secret held in writing accounts of any of the magical actions and expressions, places seen or known along the way, or concepts deep and subtle. As these events emerge from the vortex of inner and outer experience, they can be captured into glyphs, held in the book on paper to be transferred to others who can receive them by reading and replicating the work described.

As I wrote this, I recalled Cath saying, "Maybe this is a secret of time travel." We both knew that there was something to it, using words as means to open the One and discover its playground and riches.

Maturity of humanity and preservation of knowledge depends on this activity, whose essence, I was discovering, is the most deep and complex secret: our written code has the ability to transport our individual minds to the mind of All. The further we travel here, the more it is confirmed that we share a great single mind that is our birthright.

We contact this One Mind of All in many ways: through love, sacrifice, music, art, theatre, dance, ritual and ceremony, or by attunement with Nature. Some traditions and ceremonies bring it forward. I went through the doorway made of words, and found the specific stability that is known when this contact is written.

It led me to its source: the oral telling, much older and more direct. When an elder tells a story of abandoned brothers who are now the stars, it is not a distant thing, a concept to be considered or a tale that is being told. The secret that the story holds comes out through our personal resonance during the hearing. The message is ultimately from the being of All, but it was held captive throughout time within the story, like a genie in a bottle. An energetic force flows out, looking to connect with the listener on a personal level. The teller may be continuing on with his story. But the listener is gripped in a personal resonant response, one that leads to a nonverbal awakening. Story's meaning enters and is matched in the listener by a personal awareness of significance. Once again, the listener is no longer alone, but held always in the arms of a universal being, participating in that greater life.

I started to see that in progressing through the telling of our human meta-story, the time comes when all story fragments and falls away.

What the Stars Hold

Old stories told of the neglected brothers. They were children who turned into stars, and shone down upon us all to remind us about them and their lives. Were they helping us find our way even though they had been abandoned and neglected, even though they had died as children and had become stars? Were they watching over us?

If we were abandoned children, then we would see those stars and remember their story and we wouldn't be alone, we'd know we were understood. Maybe not by our parents, but by the star boys in the sky.

Night is the time when tears look silver in the darkness; glittering, reflecting the moonlight, or in a gentle, almost unseen way, shining back to those stars the subtle trail of evidence of our humanity. The composition of the vibration of tears of sadness matches exactly the composition of the vibration of those stars that are the abandoned boys.

Angry tears of frustration and loneliness are no longer in harmony with the star boys. They burned off all that way early on, and now shine with sadness and a new feeling of nobility. For their story, and therefore each of their small lives, forever lives on, in the sky and in the collective memory. They are unforgotten and now are our guiding stars.

Even if you have never heard the story, and let's face it, most of the people on earth have not, if you have been abandoned, and have cried tears of sadness, those stars would respond to you in a harmonious silvery tone. Not comfort or pity, just awareness and understanding: "Yes, we know what this is." You could feel this even indoors at night, in the city, or in a holding room in a prison or residential school.

There are so many stars and groups of stars that hold all the human stories, all the qualities and endeavours. These each shine with the vibrations that resonate when those actions and feelings occur on earth. As the old *Book of Secrets* said, "Rare and exquisite or common and coarse, all have their heavenly counterparts, for the stars are so very numerous."

THE DISSOLUTION

I fell into a trance, thinking, "Is *this* what I've been afraid of all these years? This dissolution? The place of being where all this disappears and we're left only with the essences?" Then, I saw poetically that as essences ourselves, we rise up and up to take our places fixed in the stars. Participating in their stories, in places that have always been there, our shining counterparts.

I left the notebook open on the table, pen uncapped, and stepped outside, to look up into the starry night.

Below my feet lay bones of ancestors from so many generations, so many lands, gently glowing with inner light as if they were stones in a sweat lodge. Down, down to the core of the earth, bones of humans, animals, shells, trees, leaves, insects, all crushed together over and over again by time's inexorable wine press.

I stood upon them all.

Overwhelmed, I sank to the ground. On my knees, barely breathing, I watched the descent from the stars. Sparkling lines of light descended from the stars to touch the earth in vertical lightning, the lines visible as ropes or ladders, flashing like silver rain.

The earth was turning. Imperceptibly it positioned me just so. A star that must have been mine sent a vertical beam directly into me. Piercing my crown, straight down through me into the earth. Contact. From the base of my spine something rose to meet this light-flow that was only for me.

Then I knew what I must do. I threw my head back, and opened out my arms very wide, so the star beam could directly hit my heart. That piercing line of light pulled my heart upward until my entire body ascended, suspended on the shining beam. My legs, arms and head dangled downwards, lifeless. So I remained, between heaven and earth, where all is lost in the great cry of the heart. Did I call out, an inarticulate birth-roar?

Disoriented, I dropped to the earth, *It's not time yet,* I think. *This was just a sort of rehearsal.*

My eyes opened. Stars were in their places, the ground was normal, no longer shimmering. My ears were ringing. My throat was raw. Beside the cabin, did I catch a glimpse of something moving? Better get inside. It's a cold night.

Moy Mell, my Innisfree

Names of places layered with story, with beings and gods, kings and maidens, names of the cairns that overlook the lake, names of the great stones that have seen all times and ages, names of our past in stone and in tree. In the deep woods, through tree-eyes the overseeing beings who live forever observe the world.

When the power left, the world began to be laid to waste. In sad sorrow, our eyes and hearts turned inward. Here flourished the ladders to the otherworld, and here we began to see again the olden places. They spoke to us of their provenance, and we saw them there, in the liminal lands.

Now is the time for me to once again connect with the old ones and to hear their wisdom, to bring them back to our earth so I can heal again. I go then to my Innisfree, to Moy Mell in the dunes, and here drink the refreshing waters, and find peaceful meaning. The secret lore of the great past will feed my present and nurture the future. Listen to the songs.

At the liminal land, I may stand between the worlds, with left foot on one place, right on the other. I find my way to the land of the bards, a place to meet the ones who have passed on but still wish to be in touch with us and offer us help. Here, then, is the place of plenty, the land of the poets, the place where we find our own heart's song. It is the glowing place where the poets live forever, where they meet in the plains of honey. The sweet place. All the tenderness and heart feelings are held here with the shades of the poets and their eternal verses. To go to Moy Mell is to go into the poets' company. We see them sing and find their glow. We are not here, but *there*. Soon *there* becomes a reality while here becomes the distant dream. It is a shift into the liminal, on the rainbow bridge to plenty and beauty.

The power of naming brought Moy Mell to our continent. Ella named it so, and so it became. Now we can find it anytime, from wherever we are. There are so many who cross into this faery land, to return with tales and fantasies. Attendance here is swelling, turning impossibilities into realities. We are going close to this land that the revivalists brought to us. It is now here on this continent as I think of Yeats, whose work spread this message of beauty and the ancient bardic. For his *Lake Isle of Innisfree* is not as it seems. A real place? Perhaps, but what is inferred is much more than that. Empyrean isles were exotic islands, untouched by humanity and unchanged since the dawn of time. Remember: Empyrean, from the Medieval Latin *empyreus*, an adaptation of the Ancient Greek ἔμπυρος empyrus meaning "in or on the fire (pyr)".

THE TRAGIC CABIN

Here in the dunes of the imagination I found a makeshift cabin, a hut that could last for five or ten years, a place where anything could perhaps happen, in the right circumstances, at the right time.

As with Merlin of the once and future king, guidance came in the form of an unseen green man who treats us all to a dance of fancy, but who also brings reality of death into sharp focus.

Not the pretty death of sweet rest-in-peace dreams, but the death that we all fear to know or see, the death that brings the madness of hopeless despair.

That cabin, that place of darkness, holds only a pinpoint of light, which is all we ever need to see with, particularly when it is so very dark. The cabin is old and abandoned, feeling almost booby-trapped with sagging floorboards that could snap at any moment. It is the place of the abandoned heart.

Who leads me there? Who are the two who walk beside me, one on either side, forcing me into this room where I am made to see and feel for myself this one particular mystery.

I was led into the room and you might want to know how I got out of it.

First of all, I thought I'd prepared, but I hadn't, not for that. There were some stories and books and other materials to guide my way, but I hadn't taken them in.

Still, imprisoned in the place of no life or hope, I was alive, and this little dot of life-light was enough to lead me into my own light-filled truth. It is a truth that includes this consciousness, a product of the dark days of the current century with its wars, its destruction of the earth's species, and the imbalance of the elements. Until now they had sustained us in their balance. Now it is for us to sustain them. We must learn how.

Without entering this tragic cabin, we can't ever see. Now in medieval and renaissance times hell was this place. Yes it is hell, but our hell today is not so much a physical torture but a torture of the soul. No light means no hope. Without love or any way to contact it, we are not able to leave that dark and forbidding plain of emptiness which is beyond sorrow.

As the children said about the old abandoned mansion at the edge of town, "Don't go there. An old witch lives there and she eats children."

How does someone of good heart enter this prison of mind and spirit? Taken by a magician and his consort? Or by her own curiosity and hubris? Or by the usual internal ways through grief or sharp life pains? Or by ennui unending? Whatever the means (and they are so very many,) the room is the same. Leaving it means first learning its lesson. What is the purpose of this confinement in a well of darkest darkness, solitary isolation where your cries are heard by no one?

This is a final preparatory test. Only the body, mind, and heart are imprisoned. Only the ego identification is held here. Only the seeming self is in this place. The being, the self, may be experiencing it but it is not held here. Pain is known but it is not the totality of the experience.

Here is the key: behind it all is the watcher. Watch with the watcher's eyes, hear with the watcher's ears, feel with the watcher's heart. In this way, you are always unconfined, undefeatable. Those chosen to do this are the tiny points of light in this vast darkness. Each an eye of God.

SOVIET SCIENTIST

A vast area is as yet unnavigated or surveyed. Much like the Russian expedition that sent a manned capsule into the depths of the earth, I am working my way in. That expedition inspired a sci-fi B movie that gave the whole effort a sinister cast: "Atragon, the flying submarine that bores through the earth." I hear a child's voice, "Big-one bee, I seen it!"

Atragon, my craft, must puncture the crust of the earth and burrow down as far as possible, into layers of time's sediment, into water, gas, oil, and still deeper. In it, I discover that other completely intact earth, the planet within our planet, a place that holds secrets we stored there before we were humans. Still further inside us, there are worlds that are cosmic, and off-world, outside this planet (with its inner planet held like a matrioska doll).

In imagination freed with a cosmic view, or a bird's eye view, or the moon's eye view, the whole cosmos swirls before me. I relax in the realization that our world is a tiny invisible speck and our lives in that world are even less. Yet somehow I persist in the perception that we are greater than this speck, for the cosmic view reveals it to be so. Just as the eye contains and sees far more than its small size as a physical organ, so we as human beings each contain and experience far more than our physical size in our seeming short lives on earth.

What a joke that we think ourselves confined to this small world, as if we were in prison (and also tortured) when we're actually a perceptive organ of this vast universe, visible and invisible. It is enjoying the perception of all through All, sending our communications vibrationally throughout all worlds, in and outside of time.

This breadth of being connects through the breath. It expands into fullness through our lifetime, then collapses again as we leave this limitation as we move on in a distributed intelligence, to take part even more fully in the universe. Freed from the identification of an individuated separate self, we can function as part of this vast being, relaying perceptions, acting on behalf of this great One, the only Being. Before death we can learn to play at death, until this activity is perfected. Then we no longer live at the mercy of the tiny waves in our tiny lives, but we live in the being of the great One, as active organs and emissaries.

Because this is my mission, I am that Soviet scientist boring into the crust of the earth, looking not for oil and gas but for truth, in my own life and in the lives of those close to me.

We Are Still Here

In a dream, my essence vials are all set on the shelves, my notebooks are filled, all aligned for the future. Gathering it all together in full completion had meant only foreboding to me, and it filled me with great fear. Now I am to let it all disperse back into the universal void. Just like a Tibetan sand mandala when it is fully completed, it is to be dispersed, the sand colours mixed to brown and dull grey, carried to the sea, and scattered there.

All the ground lapis of the brilliant blue? I ask.

Yes that must go.

But the valuable ruby dust, the expensive emerald dust? I ask again.

Yes, let it go to the waves.

The quartz can go, the obsidian may go, but the diamond dust, surely that will not go?

Yes, it too will go.

And so down from precious to semi-precious to the regular sand to dust.

Then as I still dream, I watch myself disrupting the beautiful pattern, stirring the sand, sweeping it into a bowl and taking it all down to the sea. The sand was now mixed with the entire universe. From an articulated essence to an undifferentiated particle of matter, just one grain of sand among innumerable others.

I taste that now on my tongue, not sweet or salty or sour. Just something, just matter, no taste, only texture. I touch the matter from the inside of my mouth and tongue. It is neither pleasant nor unpleasant. Then I touch objects, feel clothing on the skin. It is nothing. I smell the combined essences. They are muddy, murky. It ends as not much of a smell, just neutral. I can see it all: a muddled mass, nothing can be distinguished. The shape and form are dissolved. I'm not attracted or distracted, it's not distressing nor is it interesting. Nothing to hear. The singing tones of the precious stones, the brilliant sounds of the air are all slushed together into a low white noise.

Then from some nowhere inside myself, I know: it is not gone, it is found within my memory.

And when my personal memory goes? It will be in existence still, for where did it come from in the first place? It is still there, I can go there any time.

In tears, I cry, "If it all dissolves, why create it in the first place?"

"Because! There is joy here! It is a form of love's expression."

I close my eyes. I hear an onrush like the sea as waves of ecstasy crash upon me. I am lost in luminous moving patterns, brilliant, alive and exquisite to the touch. Their celestial music sweeps through unendingly as I taste the sweetest nectar, and the scent of roses fills the inner air.

"My Sweet Lord"

A delicate song echoes down through the halls of the ancients: "Yes we are still here."

I wake. It's time to leave.

In my notebook I write:

My Book of Secrets: Dedicated to Susannah

MONSTRANCE

Nature is one living monstrance held up high before the holy procession. Behind it, the sacred beings assemble and proceed. The monstrance flashes and shines in golden splendour, a living holy rose whose unfolding petals are forever opening and closing again. The giant monstrance turns. It is a massive interdimensional wheel on which all that is, was, and ever will be has its appointed place in the moment that is forever. Its center compels us to prepare for death, the personal death that leads to immortality within the being of all.

Die before death, the Sufis tell us, urging sacrifice of the small self on the divine altar of the One, the Only Being.

No need to ask how we can abandon all that we hold dear to die at an altar on which we lose everything. Bliss guides us. We enter the true corridor, a conduit direct to the center of the Rose. Paradoxically, we return to participate again in the world, only with newfound eyes, open-heart, sacred purpose.

Pathetic activity on the surface is of no consequence, even if it does threaten our planet, the lives of species, future generations, and could perhaps culminate in the end of this particular human experiment. In the enormous and vast scheme of manifestation, there are waiting in the wings many new forms and new beings coming into life at this time.

They see the procession behind the monstrance is beginning to assemble. Musicians take their positions. Acrobats and tumblers leave off rehearsing, and stand in the moment, still and present. Large groups of holy beings from all times on all planets, some barely manifested, others with feet on the ground, come into view; assembled together, variegated yet in harmony. Old beings who have just returned from the old earth arise once more with their primal messages, and join the march. New beings, yet to be imagined or born, somehow find a way to participate as a misty cloud of floating intention, as seeds of possibilities. The folk spirits of all peoples are each grouped behind a shaman of their land.

Sun shines on the golden disc and the procession moves ever forward in sacred delight.

THE ASSEMBLY AND THE VORTEX

We may take our places in our bodies, families, communities, countries, and we are formed by these and give back to these; yet our mythic destiny is a journey that brings together the beings of old with those who are to come. Beyond all forms and histories of persons and nations lies the eternal truth of all existence. It waits outside it all like a patient sphinx whose great eyes take it all in, down through history and up into not-yet-formed futures.

I stand small before this holder of knowledge, knowing it is a gatekeeper of the temple, and beyond that further is an even greater gatekeeper. Who dares to say what is the riddle of that Sphinx whose answer opens the temple gate? In my own heart and mind, I feel a gentle but insistent telepathic probing, and the question arises into my worded thoughts: *am I truly sincere?* It surprises me. I scan myself for doubts and hesitations. Yes, doubts are present but I'm holding them like sheep in a pen, grouped together, unable to escape and run wild through the fields.

I answer the Sphinx without words but in my feeling self: *Yes, I am sincere. It is a dedication and a calling.* Then a further question surfaces, one that is perhaps more challenging. *Are you ready? Have you prepared?* Echoing through me, the words seem to ring out, sounding a tone that overtakes all other sound. The sheep in the pen bleat and move, then settle again as I quietly find the calm to know inside that yes, I am ready. My eyes had been closed. I open them but the light is too bright. I close them again. The light is still there. It isn't coming from outside but is shining from somewhere within me.

I hear a loud cracking boom. It strikes three times.

The Sphinx disappears.

I stand alone on a wide plain. This is the same plain I'd stood upon in the dream vision. The ground becomes figure, emerging as a Sphinx once more. This Sphinx isn't made of stone or sand. She has the huge head of a large lioness, eyes alive, nose twitching at subtle changes in air and vibrational atmosphere.

First the Sphinx, then others, larger than life, pop up, rising up from the sands, emerging as if being born from this earth. They are opening themselves in the air and sunlight after innumerable eons of burial.

Wings unfurl, spreading to full span. Legs stretch. The large god-creatures move slowly, testing their strengths and limits. These giants are beings seen only in art and imagination, coming from the past of humanity and our efforts at symbolic understanding. Some are fears so old they have no name but show in their forms the brutish history of people and our vulnerabilities. Monsters and great slouching demons, all assembling to the tone sounded by the Sphinx. Their voices howl and cry out, noses sniffing the air, aware of one another, aware of me, the human. As they turn their eyes toward me, I feel I must speak to them in words. They can telepathically understand but it is for me to claim my power through speech.

I see an enormous congregation of the most monstrous and variegated beings, like living statues of antiquity. Their eyes show ancient nonhuman wisdom of lizard intelligence.

I accept their attentions and thank them in thought for their kindness and caring in coming that day.

"Thank you for coming to me today," I begin, my voice quavering. "I, um, really ah, appreciate your presence here." I have to take deep breath, steadying myself, then I continue. "Ah, this afternoon. How was your journey?" This I said as they were settling down, before all of them had fully turned their faces and eyes towards me. Each has eyes that beam strange vibrations.

"As you know, I too only just arrived. I hope we haven't waited too long. Have others come to assemble you before I came here?" They shuffle but don't answer. Receiving no answer in my mind, I press on. "If not yet, they soon will. We are becoming aware that we need your ancient strength, wisdom, understanding."

I look past their great grotesque forms into their intelligent alien eyes, and gather their glance toward me once more. I am striding from left to right and back again as I speak. They are as statues, fixed calmly upon me in rapt attention.

"You must not worry that we have come to abolish you, banishing you even further away in the darkness of prehistory. On the contrary, I'm here to ask for your help and participation as we face the challenges of humanity's future…" Then I lose it for a moment. My concentration falters, and they sense that. They begin to move about a little and shuffle restlessly. Luckily a great bird expands her wings before refolding them and the brilliant colour flashes before me. I return. My concentration had been thrown simply by the contact with the attention of these great beings all at once. I pull myself together.

"You!" I say to one near the front, "You carry an ancient history of worship and communion with powers even older and more powerful than yourself. We need that strength to cooperate with our purpose."

"And you," I say, turning to a monster on the left, "Your demise was not actually planned, but still it was necessary for you to rest deeply so you could return now with fresh intensities that have not yet been spent. We trust you will join us." In this way I go on singling out some of the nearest.

"Some of you have long history stretching across centuries and millennia, others have shorter reigns ..."

I am interrupted as the sky shudders above us and a great voice speaks in deep round tones: "We also are here with you today."

Then descending in a spiral comes soul upon soul and angel upon angel.

"You have shown yourself to be true," the voice speaks, "Now we will help too."

With that, a shower of angels lands to take part. The assembly has suddenly doubled.

From the left now comes the caravan of holy souls known and unknown to the world.

We all fall into a deep silence together. With eyes closed, bodies still, we enter meditation.

Peace descends upon us all.

Eventually the great bird flies round and round, and as if on command all the beings lumber and shuffle into a wide circle which becomes wider and wider as more beings join it. Angels intersperse or fly above. One single circle as the sign of God. We all move sunwise and the rays of the sun are as a tent extending toward us all equally. In that moment, I know we are held together as a great turning monstrance of God's presence, that same monstrance I'd been shown earlier.

Once again we all stand silent, this time facing the presence of the Unknown in the circle's center. Perhaps it is the first time all these beings have ever seen one another. Their eyes move from one to the other in deep acknowledgment and exchange.

Three more booms of sound crack through space.

The center begins to emanate a power. It pulls all towards it with tremendous force. Its gravitation doesn't affect me so I am able to step back and observe. I notice that the caravan of holy ones is also standing and watching.

Rushing together, all the great old Earth beings are withdrawn into the unknown, sucked down through the central vortex. To re-emerge elsewhere perhaps, on other planets or in other times? Or are they being returned to their own time and place once more, having convened in this time for God's purpose, which I've not yet understood or determined? Then the angelic beings and souls spiral upward, returning to their places above the sun. Brilliant and luminous, the spiral sings melodies from afar as the ascent becomes more and more ethereal.

Jasmine, roses, and the finest of attars blend with sandalwood, tobacco and a musky mushroomy earth scent. This aromatic symphony is all that remains in the emptiness after the splendour of the assembly.

The center closes its portal and becomes flat again; no longer a vortex, just a flat plain. Stunned, I look toward the wise ones from the caravan, but they too are disappearing, fading away like trailing incense smoke.

Later, when recalling this circle, I remember there was one multicolored feather that floated down to me. It happened right after the great bird with enormous wingspan shook her plumage. I received it as a talisman and still have it with me always. It proves to me that this was not a dream but an actual experience. Mind you, I don't worship the feather or use it in ceremonies, I only keep it safe. Perhaps it will be needed in some way later on.

The morning after that tremendous assembly, there were still so many unanswered questions. I twirled the feather in my hand, looking at its shimmering otherworldly colours. Without thought or even questions, I went over the events in sequence, fixing them in my mind. A wind of new consciousness lifted me out of myself and showed me yet another point of view. From above, I saw the wide large circle on the vast earth, while in its center was the vortex. To my astonishment, I saw that this all formed into an eye. The entire assembly looked for all the world like one great eye and the dark vortex was its pupil, its lens. Somehow I just knew that when all those creatures went into this eye, it was not happening for the first time.

Time and Memory

When I'd sat at the kitchen table weeping, recalling all those I'd harmed either on purpose or out of ignorance, by action or by neglect, Cath had told me. "Don't worry so much about it. There is no such thing as guilt. Live instead in a kind of divine forgiveness, and after that you might find you're able to live in peace, forgetting even the forgiveness. Let's do what we can from here."

Lighting a single candle together, we offered loving profound apologies to all, known and unknown to us both. Then I knew it had been done. As a seal, Cath took a small feather and a lock of my hair, bound them together with red thread dipped in the candlewax, hung it at the window for a week.Later, she came over and buried it forever.

After the ceremony I looked up my notes on one of the sessions with Gwyneth in my notebook:

"Each of us has to find our own way into this sorting room, where on one side are memories to be preserved and saved, and on the other painful past experiences best left unrecalled. Don't hold them close to the breast, like nursing a rabid stray dog or succubus.

"Life demands continual progress forward in time.

"Yet time doesn't actually exist. The one devoted to the search for the truth and meaning that life holds can't be held in only one time. The time barrier is released in sacred ceremony or by meditation. Remembering experiences in the liminal imaginaire helps fix time in another sense as a flexible framework for experience."

I remembered how she had said that our purpose in time is to overcome time. To trick time into thinking you are in one place when with the power of thought you transpose yourself into other realities simultaneously. Somehow I hadn't written this down in my notebook.

"Thought is the true time machine." I recalled her telling me. "We have this inner technology built in, part of the basic set. Our DNA triggers this activation when our thoughts are no longer guided by emotions, mind, and physical reaction. It comes to us seemingly from the outside, when we set foot on the meditative path. By meditation, I'm not just referring to the sitting meditation we are so familiar with, but also other forms. Some of these are the meditation in action, the Dreamlife, the sacred dedicated life, the wildly active intuitive madzub life, the creative life offering interplay with God."

So it was that life carried on, moving me forward, letting go of the past. But not the whole past. I didn't want to be completely unmoored. There were positive memories of those significant times in life when change and learning combined to prepare me for even more of life's demands. I kept my book of memory filled with the pressed flowers that would always remind me of sunlit meadows and carefree pleasures. And having let go of fear, I found the essence of mother love.

GREAT ESSENCE: GENTLE TENDERNESS

I hum an old song of birds nesting for the night, and all the little babies are sleeping, wrapped so gently in soft covers and furs. Our hearth-fire's flickering warm flames throw a glow so soft onto the walls here at home. *Bye baby bunting. Shush shush little one shush.*

The mother says, "Whatever your worries and fears, hungers and sadness, I am always and forever your own true loving mother. Through all time and in every way I will bring you the flowers of spring, the milk and honey of the sweetest day. I will show you where to find strawberries on the mountain path. I hold you, rock you, carry you, kiss you, smile to you and teach you all the words that you will ever need. We will play together all the games that you love. I will sing to you songs that I make up just for you right this minute. I will tell you all the stories of our whole family. I will never ever leave you. That is the deep pledge of the mother's heart. And as you grow, pushing me aside with tantrums, betrayals, lies, ungratefulness, I know it is only growing pains. I had those too with my own mum. You may think it is a serious reality that means you need to be selfish and cold, but I don't take that as the truth. For to me now and always, you are that little one who I hold so precious, so delicate.

I wrap you in this mother love. Primal animal power holds me to you in fierce protection, as fierce as a lioness licking her cub's wide face, her large broad tongue drying all tears."

My heart's well is filled to the brim with all the mothers' tears, all cried at the hopeless inability to protect our babies from all the world's dangers and sorrows, tricks and harm. In all the cells of my body comes a great and tendermost weeping. Gentle simplicity is so easily lost, hidden, unseen. We grow out of it, become harder, lose the softness. We put on cold faces, place armour over the heart.

When I dip my bucket in the well, these tears overflow to splash upon the stones. I dry them, yet still more come to wet the hard stones again and again. After a long while the stones come alive to sing their lament, a heartbreaking melody from long-ago-generations.

The baby sleeps in the basinette. Tenderly, tenderly, gentleness tiptoes in, and joins the circle of kind fairies, for yes there are fairies who are also kind. They croon an even-more ancient melody of old, so sweet that it can be barely heard over their breath. An atmosphere of almost unbearable feeling expands sensitively in the notes of the ancient tune. The song is in the old language, and it means: *By our song you can hear we are the mothers of old. Sleep now shush now, listen to our lullaby, and sleep, little one, sleep.*

All mothers hold all the babies in all the world beneath all the stars. Animals, seedpods, eggs, spores, and rhizomes.

The last essence collected now is only this tenderness of the living human heart.

SAYING GOODBYE

How did I know it was time to leave the dunes? My heart told me. I had been collecting essences, doing my esoteric experiments and writing my *Book of Secrets* without any sense of time's passing. I had, in a sense, fallen out of my own story.

It wasn't a freefall but I had less and less handle on the time and space we normally experience. I believe I've noted this accurately, and I've included several examples here so you can know how it was.

On my way to Moy Mell, I walked along the beach at twilight. Birds circling overhead drew my eye to mounting clouds on the horizon. Seeing the clouds, I felt a shift in my heart, a turning inside, a full acceptance, and I just knew.

Then suddenly it was over. I looked around at the driftwood shacks, the others living here, the struggle, the poverty, the melancholy, the whole thing and I said out loud to myself, "What on earth am I doing here?" The spell had broken, I was becoming free.

The night before, in a dream I was writing down a contact number, but the numbers in my mind were not the numbers my pen was writing. I thought 7 and my pen wrote 13. I worried I was losing my mental capacity. Then I wrote a name, my name, instead of a number. I felt I was coming through the maze. When I woke, I thought I might be ready to leave.

"So you'll be leaving us soon then?" Martin said as I joined them for dinner that night.

Was the shift that visible? I hadn't said a word to anyone about it, and had hardly put it into words myself. "Yes, I suppose I am."

There was no time to lose. I couldn't leave my cabin fast enough. Packing, goodbyes, arrangements, and soon I was on the bus, going to Cath's place for a bit, then back into the wide world of life once more.

I had packed my own translation of the surveyor's notebook, along with all my notes, cards, and charts. Before I left the cabin, I took the original surveyor's book from my knapsack and returned it to the rough shelf where I'd first found it. Turning to the open door, I stepped out onto the sundrenched sand, striding toward the sea. I faced the wide water, opened my arms to the sky and gently stepped along the shoreline.

In the distance, I saw Gwyneth, my wise friend and teacher, with her clam bucket. She waved to me and I ran right into her embrace.

"So you are on your way now," she said, matter-of-factly. The world around us shimmered and dissolved. I closed my eyes to regain my bearings, for in that flash I'd suddenly glimpsed the reality.

It had all been me! Somehow my own projected creation had spun out the entire drama without my conscious knowledge or awareness.

Even my meetings with Gwyneth had been part of this elaborate scenario. The wisdom she shared gave me a roadmap to further unfold the inner world into outer. Finally, understanding began to dawn. I saw that like a rose or anemone opening unendingly, the exquisitely delicate unfoldment of the soul drew to it all it needed. And more: all that is hidden is revealing itself as it is creating itself.

She said simply, "Now you understand."

I was speechless. She came with me a little ways along the path up through the dunes toward my emptied cabin. I had to catch my bus. Martin was ready, waiting at the doorstep. I lifted my knapsack, he took the duffelbag, and we set out for town.

When I had first come to the dunes, I'd looked out the bus window at the landscape around me: it was all lifeless and grey to my eyes. Now as I was leaving, even the smallest bit of dust danced with life force. I loved it, I loved it all. As the bus drove along, I slipped once more into the familiar place where the universal voice of my soul sings thoughts from far and wide. My closed eyes saw another journey, another travel.

My life's moments moved like diamond sand grains in the sea wind, rising together to form ever-shifting patterns and monumental dunes. The sand moved to reveal long-buried debris and hidden treasure, then flowed back to cover what once had seemed so real and permanent.

That was years ago now. I've spent the rest of my life integrating all that I learned, felt, and discovered in those golden magical days in the dunes. I often return in reverie, and as I turn the pages of my *Book of Secrets* I scarcely recognize the words as having come from me.

My cabin was taken by the sands after I left it. No one new came to stay there and it soon fell to the power of the sands and the sea winds.

HEART'S SONG

I had wanted to join with dancers who perceive and express kinaesthetically, with actors willing to try anything, with musicians able to improvise and with artists who follow their divine inspiration. I heard the call of mystics and dervishes, intellectuals, and free-ranging scholars. I was stifled and couldn't breathe, and cried for help. I found a way out, the hard way, because I didn't yet have the courage or the individuality developed to stand up for myself freely and say without guilt, shame or self-consciousness: "This is who I am, this is what I want."

Because I didn't have the wherewithal to do that, Life did it for me and to me. Out of that turmoil I was taken to the dunes for healing and recovery. There was no help for me in the patterns of normal life. I was not able to reduce my scope to a limited field, particularly in the emotional weight of what I now see was postpartum depression compounded by grief. Without even my baby to hold and love, it was as if I, too, were stillborn.

Life lost its colour. I drifted empty and useless. My arms were useless if there was no one to hold. My voice was useless with no one to sing to. I dulled myself with TV and stared at it as if it would give me life but it only reinforced the long empty evenings.

"Meditation would be good for you," they said, but I found sitting with eyes closed as useless as watching TV. No bright light, no opening, no awareness, not even the nothing I had read about. So my days spun themselves out endlessly before me. I was often sick with terrible muscle aches, or pain in my chest, or massive headaches that lasted for days. My eyes became highly sensitive to light and I often needed to wear dark glasses, even in the house. Not that I went out much. Fall, winter, spring were all the same to me. Not much registered. I napped during the day and paced at night. I didn't cry exactly but sort of moaned around, and then seemingly by itself, something started to shift.

I remember the moon was full. I was, as usual, walking around the place in the night. I looked through the window and was sure the full moon was looking at me. I just stared at it. I felt a clarity, a slight sense of contact. You might say I was interested, in a way. "Jewel of the night," I thought to the moon, "Jewel of the night." It was a beginning, and in that gentle moonlight I began to emerge, like a night-blooming flower.

From that night forward, I gradually began to feel better. I started going with Cath to the Essence Atelier and connected with the class there. I became interested again, discovering folklore and mysticism, alternatives and dreams. I felt I needed to focus only on those matters, not to rejoin the world of the average people and their workaday lives. I needed to live always with the door opened into the other world. If the liminal wasn't activated, I felt I would die, and for me the other side was far more alive than this world.

I was given a new life with understanding of the darkness we all carry.

Looking back at my experience in the dunes I could see that the baby and the impression of the loss of the baby was shown in all the worlds, in all the episodes I was seeing, dreaming, and participating in. Whether physically, in thought, in mind or in dream, I was forever communicating with my dear sweet Susannah. Susannah, my baby, was in all worlds.

I'm still not sure how much of this actually happened and how much was in my imagination. I know now that even if it was visionary without any earthly manifestation, it did actually happen.

I learned to see outside the limited vision of physical eyes alone, and to hear far beyond the range of human hearing. The tones and sounds of this unknown are now part of my everyday sensorium. In a natural way, they hook up into the greater universal sounds of the cosmos, and down into the tiny sounds of cells and unseen atom particles. All my senses are reformed in this way.

These accounts all point toward one undeniable expression of experience: my desire for release, whatever form that may take.

Our poets give over to the bardic life and pour out the images and stories as fast as the whiskey pours in. Our mystics fly through all the worlds beyond the barriers of time, space, and the speed of light, in the intoxication of the divine wine. Our shamans dream-travel and shape-shift to bring back wisdom from the ancient plants, animals, and earth spirits. Our wise women and men give counsel and compassion to all in daily life, through a continual stream of divine love.

Such command of the stars comes only with the greatest self-sacrifice. Tales abound of those who have gone beyond our stark denuded earth into the golden earth. They did so through self-sacrifice, by offering their lives entirely for whatever purpose was required. Whether initiated or not, their garments are dyed with ochre, the color of the ancient swami order, the color of the Golden Earth.

Carol Sill

Notes from Training sessions with Gwyneth Nesta

During my time at the dunes I had several intense meetings with Gwyneth Nesta, the wise woman whose help was invaluable. Included here are notes I wrote after some of these transformative sessions.

The Inner Body

I started feeling crazy and confused. I ran to Gwyneth's, anxiously knocked at her door. She hadn't been expecting me, looked disheveled and a trifle annoyed, but she let me in. After I poured out my thoughts, she told me, "Don't worry. You're going backwards to retrieve some valuable lost materials. This is a positive sign of progress. Did you think it would be easy?"

Sniffling into my handkerchief I smiled in spite of myself.

She continued, "Look inside. See? The entire game can be condensed into a single grain of sand."

I nodded, following her thought.

Forcefully she said, "Remember this: Pick up that sand grain with a pair of tweezers and really look at it. Then plant it inside you and it will become a pearl."

Listening, I felt an inner shift. I realized that with this clue I'd be able to do this work after all.

"What did you think I meant by that?" she asked.

"This is shaman advice, right? It is to take your object of study and to plant it inside yourself. But not literally. You don't actually swallow it."

She smiled.

I continued, "So, all the essences mean nothing to us if they aren't taken into a human being. That's where they're absorbed. That's where they transform and catalyze. They become translated into the language of your own personal being and life path. In that way, you become it."

"Yes, you understand. Do this, and the path to the Universal Self opens out. It's not a concept, you see, but a way."

"I know we don't swallow them, but how are the qualities taken in?"

"Innerly, in many forms and names, each according to their vibration. When you open to them, they show you. And don't be fooled. Something coarse may yield a different effect when you take it in, or if it's mixed with others."

"I've seen this with the essences. The base notes are complemented by middle and top. Always. Adding top notes reveals the purpose of the base notes as fundamental vibrations."

"Yes. The universal expansion and expression of these fundamentals goes on forever, and the additional notes of top and mid (or heart) are also never-ending. These combinations have been set to run perpetually."

"But I'm afraid. What if I become overwhelmed and lost in the living cosmic sea of space. The glimpses I've seen terrify me. What if I never get back?"

"That's a fear overlay you will need to penetrate. Pinpointing consciousness through the third eye is helpful. You can use your third eye as an insight laser. It can cut through the thick layers of physical and emotional pattern, in both sound and form."

This was exactly the advice I'd been looking for. A technique! I wanted to immediately write it in my notebook before I forgot, but in a past session she'd stopped talking as soon as I took out my pen. I listened intently, hoping I'd be able to remember after the session had ended.

"And here's a little more for the next phase. It might help you to know about this in these early days. There are inner senses that are mapped to our outer senses. When they come into play this is what happens: the seeker finds a sort of body to function through. It is a personal body that you can use to navigate the cosmic sea."

I had to interrupt. "Wow. I've heard stories of this, but thought it was a metaphor."

"Oh not at all. This body connects to your earth body in many ways, first by beams of the chakras and also by the inner senses. Their location is the pineal gland, an organ shared by both inner and outer bodies."

She touched my forehead, then moved her hand to touch my heart center.

"Here also is the inner heart. This sacred heart is where wisdom and compassion find their home, and in connection with the hearts of all they renew the world."

"Wait a minute. An inner body? Are you telling me that a person can command another sort of individual self? Kind of like a vehicle?"

"Exactly, and this seeming individual may come and go at will. We've used these bodies for eons. Some have found ways to retain these bodies in the inner realm and return to access them again in subsequent earth incarnations.

"Have you noticed the voice that comes while writing your *Book of Secrets?* I know you mentioned you've felt as if you've come into the voice."

I nodded, yes.

"That voice has a body. You can discover how to use that body. It is now yours; it may have been created lifetimes ago, by yourself, by another or by a group, who knows?"

"That's just like when I arrived here in the dunes! Someone said: 'That cabin is empty, you can stay there.'"

"Yes, like that. It is an empty shell until it's once again furnished and inhabited."

"I think I have had a bit of that experience. When that waiting shell comes to life it seems to turn things around, there's a reverse."

"What do you mean?"

"I don't sense that I inhabit it, I feel it begins to inhabit me. When I work on the *Book of Secrets* a being far more powerful, wise, and advanced than I am seems to guide me. My thought experiments come to conclusions I could never reach on my own. I couldn't even conceive of the experiments myself. Yet I somehow know."

"Now, you can prepare to command the entire vehicle, the full body, not only the voice or the thought. Being here in the dunes is wonderfully conducive to this kind of inner process. There's nothing to stop the process of connecting with the ancient wise of the ages. All the illuminated souls wait for our contact in order to shower gifts to humanity. This work is more necessary now than ever."

That night I wrote down as much of the conversation as I could remember.

EXPERIENTIAL ARTIFACTS

I knocked on her door at our usual meeting time. She met me with the question that often began our sessions: "Why are you here today?"

She liked me to declare the topic clearly at the beginning. I'd written it out so I'd be prepared. Not wasting our time in chit-chat, we started the mechanism to working right away.

"I'm here to excavate artifacts that have been long buried down through the ages," I answered.

"Excellent. What are they and how do you do this?" she asked, pointing her attention directly toward me.

"They are experiential artifacts," I said, reading from my notes. "I dig them out of my own DNA and turn them into words after I experience them in my inner senses." I held the notebook I'd brought with me to show her, but she waved it away, and guided me to the sitting area.

"Ah, the old noble undertaking. Please, sit." We settled into one of her two small armchairs. The side table between us was at the ready with our usual tea, brandy and figs.

"Now," she said with eagerness as she handed me my tea, "What's your approach?"

"I was thinking of detangling the strands and reading their inner codes, not in a scientific way, but in the way of the weavers of old."

"Yes, good… life's complexities can sometimes only be sorted out by hand."

"Exactly. You know, taking the messy knotted mass and teasing out the threads. Laying the pieces out straight, organizing them by colour and material and thickness. Then rolling them into a ball to keep them all tidy."

She nodded. "This is ancient work that the shamans and wise ones knew. I didn't take that route. Each of us follows our own path toward the same goal." She'd repeated this many times before. We both knew it was a signal that we were entering the shifted space again.

As if she heard something outside, she suddenly changed the subject, or seemed to, saying, "To discover the use of a plant for healing is a western way to describe the relationship with the being of that plant. That being is nuanced and many-faceted; never think it can be categorized in a non-living way. It would be like saying you discover the "usefulness" of another human being, or the "use" of an angel to produce money. The true ways to refer to these encounters are music, art and love, or the poetry of communion."

Without looking at my notes she'd intuited some of the study I'd brought to show her.

"That's exactly what I have been trying to get at," I replied. "I've been looking into the botanical notebooks of Hilma af Klint. I saw how her work completely changed as she opened up to receive the inner vibrations. She entered deep relationships with the plants she focused upon. When this happened, her precise botanical illustrations moved to full intuitive abstraction. Creating the botanical illustrations revealed the energy frequencies and poetic abstractions of the plants she studied."

"Have you seen for yourself what was shown to her in this beautiful process?" she asked.

"I wish I could understand it. Her notes refer to something beyond language as I know it. The symbols in the illustrations are abstract," I said.

"Perhaps if you relax and read intuitively, with the eye of inner understanding," she suggested. "Esoteric systems are direct, profoundly precise, and transferred in symbol and contact."

We were silent for a few moments. She sipped her brandy, I took my tea, she offered a fig, taking one for herself.

Then she continued, saying, "Try examining the complexity with simplicity and an open heart. Focus on one aspect only."

"So, one aspect at a time," I nodded, "Right. I get it. A deeper relationship happens when that point of focus becomes a door or pathway into itself, like the plants did for Hilma."

Gwenyth nodded, "Yes. Use harmonious correspondences. Enter into a vibrationally-matched dance. Let play happen when your essence is in full contact with the essence of the point of focus. Together you both create and perceive a loving relationship. You meet one another essence to essence, as it were."

"So it is love?" I asked.

"Naturally," she smiled. "You see, there can be no gathering of the essences or understanding of them without this Love. I warn you, it can be challenging to engage with some of the darker ones, and it can be difficult to return after engaging with the light beings."

"I remember reading about your experience of that in your *Book of Secrets*. But at the time, I didn't know what it really meant."

She looked at me then with infinite kindness, saying, "As human beings it is our right, duty and privilege to make sense of what we experience. I brought my story out for the sake of others, pupils like you." She chuckled and raised her glass.

"We are to love and honour this seen and unseen creation through the power of our attention." She paused, and thought for a moment, then added, "Some say it can only be done by creative expression. I say our creativity is the way we make love to the universe."

At this, laughter caught us by surprise. She started laughing, then the joy just burst out of us both.

INITIATION TRAINING

"Welcome," she opened her arms. Her warm greeting helped me feel at ease. "I'm looking forward to a useful and interesting session. Please come in now, sit, and let's begin."

After only a little bit of small talk, we got into the topic of writing. I'd given her the account I'd written the week before and was a little nervous about her response.

"First, do you have any questions before we start?" She seemed to be in a state both calm and agitated, and I wasn't sure how to respond, so I just launched in with something that occurred to me.

"When I write in my *Book of Secrets* I enter a realm of thought that we've shared down throughout the ages. I glimpse the great library of our akashic record."

"Exactly. Now to go further, we look to the third eye." As she tapped her forehead, her eyes flashed toward me.

"Is this the same as the pineal gland?" I asked.

"Some say so. They say that this is where our interdimensional consciousness expands and exchanges information and being with all other life, known and unknown to the world. We've talked about this, remember?"

"So when I write, this concentration of the eyes is actually a kind of activation of the third eye?"

"It may be so for you. This communication centre opens our awareness far beyond the physical and metaphysical. Actually far beyond the known world. It's a key to the knowledge of past, present, and future. Embedded in our brain it is poised when we're ready to begin transmission, in your case, writing. Contact to and from the human realm occurs here, through those who've discovered or awakened this particular key. It's a sacred code. Down through the centuries it has been passed along from master to disciple since the beginning of time."

She closed her eyes, and then began to speak in a voice that was a little deeper and more measured than her normal conversational tone and rhythm.

"Those who've been selected to communicate these messages of love, harmony, and beauty are the souls who are willing to sacrifice everything in this divine cause," she said softly.

I fell into a sort of dream as she continued on. "Please listen carefully. Those who embody this message are being trained to receive a higher charge in the vital field."

"How does this happen?" I asked.

"It's already happening for you, between us, now. To be in Nature, to be still, to have few worries or regrets, these are the prerequisites for that level of esoteric inner training. You are well-suited."

"Then the communication happens?"

"Yes. Once that training has completed, the seeker becomes a messenger. Not the only messenger, but one of the caravan of dedicated messengers."

"And this is why we begin each session with the dedication *Toward the One, The perfection of love, harmony and beauty, the only being, United with all the illuminated souls, who form the embodiment of the master, the spirit of guidance.* It's because we are connecting to this stream of messengers."

Nodding in affirmation, she continued: "I want to use the time that we have together to speak about the need of the day. In these times there are many challenges. We pray they will be resolved through the agency of inspired and enlightened individuals: people willing to enter the great effort of saving the human experiment. They have connected their intuition to a source of infinite wisdom. They are becoming inspired to act and benefit the world today.

"There have been many in the past who with all good intentions have paved the way to hell. We are living in such hell now. Disconnected from all that maintains our natural humanity we find ourselves adrift - far from our natural communion with nature, and far from ourselves. Each of us must take the vow to protect and keep what little is left of the beauty of humanity and the wisdom in the world."

As we sit together in silence, I see before me a flash of divine vision. We're transported to an eternal cave in some liminal depths where all can be seen. This cave is lined round with many eyes, eyes on the ceiling, eyes on the walls, eyes on the floor of the larger chamber. Above is an open oculus. We stand inside this cave and look up through that opening.

In former times it was a smoke hole, so people in the cave could light a fire and the smoke would rise out through the hole and disperse in the air. Inside the cave, which is a living being, men and women were reborn in an ancient ceremony. There have been many such ceremonies in the past. It felt like an old esoteric secret. In the Koran, the seven sleepers were in this cave.

"It really *is* what you think it is," she said.

"In the cave, I was asking you in thought, 'does this make sense?' Or am I just making up something that blurs together varied forms from times past to times present."

"You know how to do this."

"Do you mean that I can find the words that come from here, or from somewhere that I have never gone before?"

"You can fly free here just as Milton flew free into the vastness of the imaginaire, for when you're blind to this world you may receive the vision of the world beyond."

"But there's a censor in my mind telling me, "Don't say that, say this. Don't do that, do this. Don't think that, think this."

"Try it this way. Tell it to me as if it were a story. Take me through it."

"That censor is the dog that stands at the gate, the fairytale dog with eyes as big as saucers. He's like a great Dane and he stands in front of the gate that is the doorway to the cemetery. I walk through the gate, and onto the path. I come to the family mausoleum of someone I have never met. A tall white door that has been barred stands between two pillars. The dog is behind me now. I thought there would be another dog at the door of this family mausoleum, but there isn't.

I recognize that this is a place that has been calling me to come, to open the door and descend the staircase into the great hall where merriment continues night and day. It has been so for thousands of years. For some reason, the family to whom this monument was placed on that soil in Italy long ago never existed. This is simply a façade, a trick. I know this is no ordinary mausoleum, it is a gateway to the unseen world. Once you go past the carousing revels of the beings who for centuries inspired the Vikings and all the bards (this could be why the dog was a "Great Dane") there's an even deeper world to explore.

This mausoleum which is found in "Italy" has counterparts throughout the western world. It's possible in many old cemeteries to find one such Gateway. I know, this sounds like fantasy story about things that I imagine. But I feel I am there at this party, this ongoing feast that is the celebration of life itself. The next level comes after we leave the great table. We go behind the curtain into the other rooms, then out into the garden. A manicured garden is to the right, but we choose to enter the forest on the left. Walking through the forest on the beautiful path, we hear birds that have been singing forever. The branches of the trees hold jewel droplets as if they were rain drops. The moon in the sky calls to our hearts, and within a tide of love we rise."

I paused, surprised by the flow of my words. She smiled, and nodded. Then as she spoke in a new rhythm, I was taken into a trance.

Her voice tells me, "This is the sort of traveling that we can do if we wish. All places, whether real or unreal, are available to us. If we have the ability to fly we are ready to go all over the world, now and back to the time before the western peoples set out to destroy this world. Our holy people who are shamans and wise women flew to meet one another to connect across time, space, and language. We'd fly to locations where we would learn new ceremonies. We'd offer our rituals on the doorways of the unknown peoples. We'd travel to new planets.

"We'd go past the dimension of time. We sit today in a circle that has a space for you. Join us now. Our circle is serious. It is sincere and as old as time, as old as humanity. Here in our circle, the fire sits before us and we help one another. For we know that together with the help of our unseen brothers and sisters, we can influence the core of our planet.

"Besides, there are many beings who have not ever incarnated on Earth. These ones, these noble ones, these participants in life without form, they are also our allies and our helpers as we transition into the greatest century known to humanity."

In trance, I heard one speak, saying, 'Don't let the pain and suffering of our first pangs threaten you, or make you lose heart.'

Another said, 'Don't let your desire for any set belief structure stand in the way of your expression and growth.'

Another looked at me and said, 'Through art we can leap over the wall of religion and taste the fruit that grows in the wilderness of creativity.'

Then a whirlwind of words came in a joyful, hilarious, interdimensional Joycean swirl. I zoomed in on words spelled and misspelled in many levels of resonant meaning and playful joy, in various languages, homonyms, antonyms, anagrams, puns, substitutions, some more perfect than any word I may have thought I had selected. For secretly inside each word are 15 or 25 or even more other words all vying for position to come forward as The Word.

I realized that we individual people are in the same situation: each of us holds innumerable people inside, all going forward, pouring themselves forward, each vying for a position as the voice of being, the only one. We find in ourselves our own Khumba Mela.

Reaching forward, we seek that one true being who will guide us and keep all these parts of the self held true and magnificent.

My ears were ringing. I opened my eyes to see she was waiting for me. She walked me to the door.

"Thank you so much," I murmured, in tears. "I have no idea what to do." Returning to my limited self, I felt an immense fragmentation of consciousness.

"You will know. Trust."

"Do I dare to imagine a world that is so different from the one I grew up in?"

" It is imagined bit by bit and step by step. There is no sudden conversion. We build upon what we already have. Remember, the messengers are embedded in all walks of life, in all names and forms, in every direction, in every location, and in every intention. These are the surrendered souls. No words can tell the joy and completion felt by those who offer their all so that humanity may survive."

I left the session stunned, awash in thoughts. My ears were still ringing, but my thoughts returned to earth, my feet felt firm on the ground.

PEP TALK

I rushed in with emotional intensity, having so much to sort out since the last session. I needed to express my doubts about my *Book of Secrets*, and there was something else that I felt needed to come forward.

"Okay, shoot," she said, as I sat down.

"I'm worried. So many before me have written and expressed this, and far better. Why should I bother with my puny little effort?"

"Oh is that all?" she smiled. "The answer is so simple. Because it is an outpouring of love, a way to find out more about our human condition. Remember, you are nothing more than a sensor, a point of awareness. But being a sensor, a receiver, may not be what you imagined. That sensing is only one side of the connection. You are also to give back to the source; send it back to the source of your sensory experience." She paused and looked me in the eye, waiting for my response.

"Okay, what I'm getting is this: My receiving is only one half of it all. I have to give something back too. I'm also to return the contact with love, gratitude, and appreciation. I think I already know this."

"Stay with me here. Your gratitude can be best expressed in a creative form, such as your *Book of Secrets*."

"Why? I don't get that."

"Because from an earthly point of view don't you think that it is too much to be saying "thank you, thank you" day and night with each and every sensation, sight, sound, smell, taste, experience? "

I had to smile. "Well, yes, it would really get in the way of normal human life if we added a conscious gratitude response to every sensation."

She chuckled at the thought, too. "Exactly. But how can any one of us take for granted the incredible sensorium we live in? Not to mention the fantastic imaginaire! Remember, that is the wonderful akasha."

She went on, "Think of it! When the unseen world comes into view, we are humbled at the vastness of all that is yet to be known."

I thought about how we're tiny and limited here on earth, so truly small, and our lives barely register in the scheme of all, like a flash or flicker. And at the same time, we contain multitudes of worlds and beings and can commune with them any time at will.

'That's it," she said, for she'd heard my thought.

"So, my gratitude and love can be shown in a creative, condensed way? Like my *Book of Secrets?*"

"Exactly."

Suddenly I understood. "And that's a way the Creator is extended through our human agency!"

"What greater gratitude can there be? Our humanity is truly fulfilled in the act of all-absorbing creativity."

"Right! All we need to do is work and play together."

"Remember, you can be an agent for the outpouring of love."

Realigned, reassured, I thought, *Well from that point of view, it's a natural next step. I'm encouraged. Because even if many before me have written about this, and far better, as an agent for the outpouring of love I add my own voice to the chorus. It's natural, like the singing of the birds.*

PERCEPTIONS

"Welcome," Gwyneth said. "Let's sit and just take a moment to tune in now to the Source."

I sat in my usual chair, she sat in hers, and we closed our eyes for a few minutes.

She began, "I know you wish to learn more so you can express once again the exquisite realm of the fairy and imagination. The liminal."

"Yes," I replied eagerly, "I've been so inspired by Ella. She moves a power that might be called mythological ..."

My mind slipped as she glanced away, then changed the topic suddenly. She often did this, especially when I had a definite idea of what she'd be talking about. "We all need community. Of course you'll need others, and yet it is in solitude that our hearts find their deepest rest."

I nodded in agreement. We looked out the window, scanning as gentle clouds hugged the horizon beyond, far across the water.

She spoke now of her own experience, saying, "Seeing the water gives my eyes such rest. When I look into the sea my eyes pour out vibrational communications. At contact with the water, when I "see" it, that water returns the beautiful exchange back to me through my eyes. At the same time I feel the sea. I smell the sea. I hear the sea and the birds of the sea. This all combines together to bring me into an intimacy the Sufis have described as Love, Lover and Beloved. The nature of creation."

I felt as if we were stepping into a dream together as I listened to the melody of her words.

"I've learned that my senses are not only perceivers of the world around me. They don't just allow me to sense the world. They also have a finer purpose, which you may also discover. It is like this: A lover gazing into the lover's eyes brings forth a loving response, right?"

"Yes," I said.

"Well this begins the delicate exchange of high frequency information. Are you with me so far?"

I nodded.

"All right. So the same thing happens when my eyes look upon any thing, person, object, or anything whatsoever. There's an exchange: a deep intersensory contact."

I waited for her to continue.

"Looking at the fire, particularly if the flame is not covered by glass, is beneficial for the eyes. Pure communication from the fire element restores the eye's natural balanced functioning. What the fire gives to the eye in yoga practice such as tratak, for example, is very healing. The eye seeks light, communicates with light. Light communicates to and through the eyes. We look for light, go towards it, and eventually learn to see the light shining in darkness. How? We can't exactly say, but our hearts know."

I thought about my work with the essences. Somehow it connected. These can be simple energetic elemental ways that the world may be restored, one person at a time, one sense at a time. The perfumers' art is an exquisite liminal communication that brings poetic balance to our senses. I remembered reading, "We are learning the secrets held in the molecules of scent, the essential compression of the purity of the vibration. The essence of the Rose, the Lilac, the Jasmine, and the essence of grasses, or as some artisanal scent developers do, the scent of the sea, the scent of soil, the scent of snow and of imminent snow or old melted snow..." The process was called a recapturing and re-invigorating retrieval of the natural human sensorium.

I came back to the present. Somehow I hadn't been listening. I tuned in again, to hear her say, "This should be our practice each day: learn to touch and allow touch and scent and taste and sound and sight to engage. It is our covenant in creation. We are not meant to be strict Puritans who don't engage in any sensuous activities. We are not meant to engage in the world of thoughts only. A narrow corridor with closed senses has its purpose but it is not the purpose of human life. Of course, for meditation and to understand inner potential we need to close the senses, to awaken the inner life. Some of my colleagues say that extended poverty of the external sensorium, where it's in a state of underdevelopment, leads to a profound expansion of the inner senses. Others see it as an impoverishment. What do you think?" she suddenly asked me, turning to face me fully.

I hesitated before I spoke what was in my heart. "We're given through our senses the ability to experience all creation in love. Maybe when we're ready to take what you've called the return journey, at that time we look within, but not until then."

"Yes, and when we do look within, there light finds us, we see the inner exquisite brilliant light. Beautiful inner sounds produce themselves within us and are heard not with the outer ear but by the ears within. Exquisite scents emerge and we experience the divine scent. We taste nectar that pours through the body, awakening even greater love. Deeply sensitive inner touch has nothing to do with the skin or the sensory touch mechanism, but is inward waves of bliss. This happens after the human instrument is developed, defined, expanded, and then purified. As you are now doing. Our senses can be fully awakened to this creative two-way communication between the seer and the seen. This nurtures and prepares us for the full experience of the inner senses."

"I think I'm starting to naturally experience my senses this way. For example, when I collect the essences, I sense they are connecting to me. Sometimes it's as if they call me, and intuitively I find them. Is this what you mean?"

"Not exactly. I was referring to the actual sight, sound, smell, taste, touch: that moment of contact without thought connected to it. A pure percept, before mind comes in to translate. Part of it is to realize that at the instant of the percept, the object of perception is also responding. It isn't so much intuition as simple pure percept, shared."

I looked out at the sea again, now with a sense of supreme peace and belonging. Then I wondered if perhaps the sea had returned my gaze with love. Once more, I found I'd tuned out from the conversation when I heard her speaking again.

"To paraphrase what Inayat Khan said: 'Everywhere I look I see Thee, everything I touch I am touching Thee, everything I hear I am hearing Thee..' We have within us the rich exquisite sensorium of the highest and finest bliss. At the same time, our outer senses are experiencing unity, the Presence transpiring through all things."

She closed her eyes, and drifted into meditation. I soon slipped out the door unnoticed.

Overhead, the seabirds flew, calling and swooping in great loops and circles, as if they were inscribing asemic letters in the sky.

BURNING, KARMA

Excited, I rushed in and we started right away.

"Lets talk about fire and water." She began. "There's no separation between the small life and the greater life. Identification of the self with only the smaller life causes so much suffering that it eventually has to just burn itself out. At that point, in this darkness, a hand is offered by those illuminated souls who've gone before. I sense that you've felt that."

"Yes, I have; like something or someone pulling me up out of the maelstrom. The farther I go from that swirling current as I rise up, the more I see my part in its creation, my part in its continuance. As I take that hand I vow with all my heart to be free from that vortex of drama and pain."

She smiled. "Of course it's an ongoing process. There are aspects that still cling and that we still cling to, and they burn off at a different time or at another rate. All our lives, karma is burning off of us. Not only personal but transpersonal as well."

I sat attentive, listening with an open heart. It was as if my heart were on fire as she spoke.

"Ancestral karma, the karma of our race, of our country, and of Nature, do you feel it all burning?"

Nodding yes, I wasn't able to move. Fixed in my spot, I waited for her next words. As she spoke, I saw everything she described in full detail in my mind's eye.

"All this burns with us, while throughout our lives we improvise delicately with all beings in symphonic orchestration. Visions of heavens and hells, memories of childhood traumas and ideals, intimations of the future, all find their way to join in our hearts. Do you feel it now?"

And my heart burned open to become an eye and an ear and a bell.

"The awakened heart is fed by interstellar awareness and regulated by the active inner visionary realization of the third eye. Now your heart may focus on a vast new depth awareness of life."

"So it is required that we burn off all that is no longer needed?"

"Yes. Each one of us is consumed in our own hellfires. Like rain, a loving compassion comes naturally when the clouds have so accumulated that nothing else can be done except a release of the downpour. Compassion and understanding pour like rain on the thirsty soul. In this way of love, the heart is sacrificed again and again upon its own altar."

An energetic rush of unwordable thought whirled through my awareness. It was all too much for me to take in. I had to just sit silent for a while. We sat together until the sun had nearly set; then she rose quickly and walked me to the door to say goodbye. Still in tears, I obediently left for home. Then grateful, I turned back toward her to say thank you, but it was too late. She'd already closed the door and had gone back inside.

My Book of Secrets

When I came to the end of my time in the dunes, I went to my dear and wise friend, holding the sheaf of papers in my hands.

"I have all my notes based on our work so far," I said, "They're all here. I've described all the essence, how to create or find them, and how to use them. My notebooks are here too, telling of dreams and events important to daily life. Is it true that daily life is not as valuable to the *Book of Secrets* as the distilled essentials?"

Placing a stack of papers on her table, I started right in. "Okay, here's the material about the essences." I took another sheaf of pages from my bag. "Here I have the writing about my experiences."

She nodded for me to continue.

"I have other ideas that came while I've been working on the essences." I put the third stack out. "Do I include all these in my *Book of Secrets*? Or do I pare it down to only include essences and their formulas?"

"Have you tried to find the essences of the experiences you're describing?"

It wasn't want I wanted to hear. "That's easier to say than do," I replied, a little sharply.

Just then, as if on cue, the sun poured through her cabin. I know, it sounds hackneyed. Contrived. The rays of the sun seemed to touch right into my mind, bringing the thought: *the sun shines equally on all that exists on earth. When it shines on me, I am blessed.* The appearance of the sun, so strong and vivid, completely erased my contact with her. Druid that she is, it was as if she bowed, stepped back and dissolved into the shadows at the sight of the greater one.

The rays of sun-power invigorated my confidence. I thought: "I'm writing my part of the solar story, even if it's incomplete and only a tiny aspect of the vast system." In my mind's eye, I saw this story as a whole creation in its own right, just as it is.

Lifting my face to drink in the glorious rays, I felt red-gold heat on my closed eyelids. In my third eye I sensed the powerful something that awakens the inspiration to communicate with the wise and with those far distant in time and space.

That brilliant light showed me that writing about an experience already reduces it to an essential communication. The words themselves aren't just alphabetically formed, but their marks and glyphs indicate essences. I absorbed the sun's answer: my *Book of Secrets* is solar, and, like the sun, shines on everything either directly or indirectly.

I remembered the *Book of Knowledge* that I'd pored over as a little girl. It was my grandmother's book, large and heavy-bound. An Edwardian encyclopedia containing advice for young girls, lists of animals and plants of the world, useful cuts of meat, weather, instructions on knots. Random episodes and fragments were lined up in a codex as if it included all knowledge, which of course it could not, for how can one book or poem include all knowledge?

Out loud, I asked, "Is it possible that one word on a page can refer to all that is, was and will be? I want talismanic writing: the engraved power of words that was known to the ancients."

"It is not lost to us; this desire can be your ally as you prepare your *Book of Secrets*. Be sure, though, that notations from true inner travels form the basis of your book. For that is how it should be," she declared. She showed me a weathered book and began to read:

"Here's what another *Book of Secrets* declared in its introduction:

'If you happen to be reading this now and holding it in your hand, you may think it is just another book. I dearly hope you will be able to discover its inner aspect. For as it was being written, the author was for a time taken into states beyond the limitation of everyday diurnal consciousness. Should the words appear lifeless and flat on the page, please bear with your humble author. Please remember the other world to which these words refer. If indeed it does appear over time that I have been like a child making mud cakes but serving them as if they were a delight for tea, then I myself will discover they are inedible.'"

I smiled in recognition. I felt the same. I poured out to her all my regrets, saying, "My book has no plot, and I regret that the characters are barely sketched. Ideas once introduced may not fully develop. There is no clear transition from one aspect of the book to the other, and the time and place makes no sense. But I so enjoy the entire interplay and contact from the poets who live in that node of imaginaire we call Moy Mell. They bring magical complexities into this book. The world is burning, and I sit writing about an imaginary person doing an imaginary thing in an imaginary place. How can that help? Yet I do this with such focus and sincerity that I wonder what is it then that is being done?"

She nodded. "The bardic notes down through the ages have always held together the human story. They sound through all the darkness of war, pestilence and basic human grasping for power."

"The poets of Moy Mell understand," she continued. "What you are doing is the oldest ritual, one that all poets know: leaving behind, stepping in, and in some way (for each of us it's different) opening the doors of awareness to include the others, those with whom we co-create. They wait for our contact and they don't act without our engagement. See it as a large sort of casting call, where they sit in the anteroom until you call them forward to show us what they can do. Some of them are so evolved they emanate wisdom in a glance, in a movement, or simply by their presence. But first they must be called, with respect and humility."

"I sensed that," I said. "The process always surprises me. When I connect with them, their great sense of humor and playful love overturns my awe."

"Exactly! This is the play! This entire space is nothing but an emanation of love for humanity. Describing this place or akasha is part of any *Book of Secrets*."

I drifted down again into my own thoughts. There is a quest; there is a place to go. Life and its challenges wear the personality down into powerlessness and weakness. That's when a ray of light from the sun can appear at the bidding of the wise. Then the wise fade away, and the light of the sun communicates hope, life and purpose to the person who has in all humility asked for help, asked "what now?" just as I did. I had asked within, "Please help me, where do I go from here?" They say that when the cry is sincere and the seeker is ready, an answer comes immediately like a ray of brilliant golden light.

"So what happens next?" I asked.

"Writing your account uplifts you with an awareness that takes you into new ideas, but personalized. Ancient wisdom perhaps, but personalized. You understand now. The path is a personal path. It's not a vast highway where identical beings do identical things to receive identical outcomes and become identically enlightened. The path of the mystic winds its way in patterns more labyrinthine than can be imagined and with each flash at a turn or a return there's an emission of light. That's a gift to all. Now, the mystic is unaware of these flashes. Concentrating only on this path to truth, she must remain in a state of attentive relaxation to receive the next instruction.

"It seems that there is no "next" without coming to an end. An empty time is followed by new life that engages as far as the seeker will permit. The seeker who has not yet burned off or released certain clinging habits or notions may not be ready to receive the next series of instructions."

My mind took me through an old familiar personal labyrinth. *I wonder if she means me? If I am not ready?* I ask myself, why do I wonder if I am ready? This may be the question that impedes progress. Besides, no one but ourselves knows when we're ready and what we're ready for.

I noticed that she sat before me with eyes closed. Had she dozed off while I had sunk into my own thinking, or was she meditating? My thoughts in free play flowed on, more like a voice sort of singing within me than like my own mind.

"Our path, being uniquely our own, will not unfold itself in any way other than its intended directive. We always have options in our engagement with the divine playmate. Every moment the Creator is awaiting our surprise visit, and this is who we delight through our dancing. In playful love and surprising affiliations, the Creator takes even more delight than we do in the beauty, wonder, and magnificence of each moment's instant.

"As we dance together, we both create and perceive a new life: a life force not only personal but for all of humanity. The radiant love of the hearts of all: awakening to this is the divine goal.

"We know there is so much suffering, sorrow and pain in this world. This educational world. All we can do is gather our perceptions into the center of the inner being, offering it all in utmost humility to All, to the Universe, to God. We continually gather and gather every essence, impulse, perception, along with every touch, sight, sound, taste, and scent as they pour through us. We form and compress all this into the most incredible gift. This is all our sacrifice. And we confess ourselves a flash, a bubble in the stream."

It seemed we both opened our eyes at the same time. I couldn't tell if the thoughts I'd had were hers or mine. Slow and silent, she moved to gather my papers and hand them back to me. Our eyebeams glanced one another in acknowledgment, as I took the pages from her outstretched hands. She held the door open for me. I stepped into the bright light of mid-day, clasping my papers in front of me like a schoolgirl holding her textbooks.

Epilogue

After the intense explorations that were catalysed and amplified during my stay in the dunes, my life began to naturally balance itself out. That's a whole other story: how I learned to live simultaneously both here and there once I'd left the dunes.

As I write this account once again, just for this time, I am wild and free, living in the expanded consciousness of all the free spirits. The magical inner realms are wide open. I sing the songs of old, a troubadour at the court of the king and queen, where singer, song and hearer are One. I pour out my heart's song, full-throated as an Andalusian gypsy. The entire cosmos vibrates harmonies as fine as the most ecstatic angelic chorus.

In time, I built a rose garden, following the lines laid out by the wise of Cordoba, the Sufi, Christian, and Jewish mystics who were alchemists of fine perfumes distilled in the walled gardens of truth.

Now, whenever I wish, I rest in my garden of secrets. Wisteria welcomes at the gate. Jasmine's scent draws me in. The sun's rays warm the walls. Over the generations, esplaniered lemon and blood orange trees have transformed powerfully scented blossoms into fine fruit.

At the centre a fountain shimmers. In sunlight's splendour, its diamond droplets rise in extravagant abandon only to fall into the clear pool below. I pick a blood orange from the branch of an old cultivated tree. The sounds blend: the fountain, the bees, the quiet stones, a few very small birds. I sit quiet on a bench backed and flanked by exquisite roses.

This garden's counterpart is a library where encoded wisdom is preserved forever. Each *Book of Secrets* is a diamond droplet from the fountain of knowledge, dissolving in the pool of wisdom.

I stand and walk out of the garden into the brilliant morning light. Taking a large bite of the tangy blood orange, I eat the sun.

Acknowledgements

Thank you to everyone who helped me in this work. James K-M, for the artful book cover, his keen reading and encouragement to go wherever it takes to expand my writing. Donaleen Saul for insightful, skilled editorial. Ann Mortifee, whose loving assessment brought the story forward. Diane Feught for taking the work seriously. Mariette Berinstein for the space to write on the Sunshine Coast. Carol Sokoloff for the quote from her Lake O'Hara song. Joe Clare for his kind support. Thanks also to friends who inspired me along the way; to my first readers who tried to plough through the mess of the first draft; to nanowrimo for the kick-start and Isabella Mori for turning me on to nanowrimo. Special thanks to the incomparable Sufi, Shamcher Bryn Beorse, for taking me to the Dunes in conversation and through his book, *Fairy Tales are True*. I'm grateful to the poetic souls of Ella Young and Daphne Dunn. I should also mention books on the Dunes by Norm Hammond (*The Dunites, Elwood:Spirit of the Dunes*) and Luther Whiteman (*Face of the Clam*). Finally, I offer my reverance, homage, and gratitude to the work of all perfumers known and unknown to the world.

Carol Sill, Vancouver, 2017

About the Author

Carol Sill is a writer, editor, and publisher living in Vancouver, BC, with the abstract artist James K-M and their beagle, B.

A grandmother of two, she has been engaged in the practical application of ancient spiritual wisdom for over four decades. Her other books include *Human Ecology: Notes on the Sacred Element Work*, *Documentary Print*, and *Letters: Shamcher Beorse and Carol Sill*.

Carol was the editor of Ann Mortifee's acclaimed best-seller, *In Love with the Mystery*. In addition, she has republished several books by her Sufi teacher, Shamcher Beorse, including *Fairy Tales are True*, *Every Willing Hand*, and *Planet Earth Demands*. She currently manages the Shamcher Archives.

More info on this book can be found at www.attars.shamcher.com

94154656R00124

Made in the USA
Columbia, SC
22 April 2018